SCARRED

URBAN FANTASY

BOUND BY SHADOWS
BOOK ONE

ANN GIMPEL

CONTENTS

SCARRED

BOUND BY SHADOWS, BOOK ONE

Urban Fantasy

By

Ann Gimpel

Tumble off reality's edge into a cruel world where only the perfect are valued.

Copyright Page

BOOK DESCRIPTION, SCARRED

Magic runs strong in me, but power isn't enough.

Magic confers an unnatural beauty on everyone with talent. Everyone except me, that is. I'm a witch, to be sure. No doubt about my birthright. When I was young, Mother hid me away until I was old enough to hold a glamour to conceal my flaws.

And hold it I did for many a long year until I grew sick of siphoning off that amount of magic on something stupid. I was a valued Coven member. Surely, they'd accept me. And my wolfie familiar. All witches have them, except most are cats or birds. Something small, manageable.

Eh. Getting off track here. The unpleasant truth was the moment I sloughed my glamour, the council held an emergency meeting. The next day, I was out on the streets. They booted wolfie along with me.

No more home. No more sisterhood. Hah. What a joke all those of years of bonhomie turned out to be. If I sound bitter, darned right I am. Bitter and moving forward.

I'll show them if it's the last thing I do.

BOOKS IN THE BOUND BY SHADOWS SERIES

Scarred, Book One
Cursed, Book Two
Promised, Book Three

AUTHOR'S NOTE

When I finished Grigori, last of the Circle of Assassin books, I surveyed my newsletter subscribers to determine what to write next. I may have gone overboard this last Black Friday, but I now have covers for three very different series. Covers are always an author's rate limiting step, so I stock up when I can.

The consensus amongst my newsletter group was they wanted the misfit witch series. A reaper series, Urban Sisters, came in second. A dystopian series, Shattered Worlds, was a distant third. Gosh, wonder if I'll ever get around to writing that one.

I love plotting out brand new series. Who will the characters be? Where will it take place? Will the world be open (e.g. humans know about magic) or closed? Will there be portals?

So many directions.

Guess I'd best get started. So far, I've written the blurb. Onward to chapter one.

CHAPTER ONE, MORGAN

Rain sluiced from leaden skies. The weather in Seattle sucked. So what else was new? I trudged along narrow byways on Capitol Hill, hoping to catch a break. We'd spent the previous night under a bridge. Surely, I could improve our circumstances. Brick buildings rose above me. Most had been converted to cheap flats—weekly rentals—which was why I'd chosen this neighborhood.

"We should leave," Zeke growled. *"Nothing to hold us here."*

He's a white wolf, and my familiar. Today, he looks more like a shaggy brown dog since a wolf would draw far too much attention on busy city streets. He shook water off his back, spraying me. I might have minded if I weren't already soaked.

"It may come to that." I buried a hand in his wet pelt

and scratched behind his ears. *"We're not leaving today, though."*

A muted yip swelled through me. He really did look pathetic. Even his ears drooped. I stopped walking and drew us beneath an overhanging balcony. It cut the rain a bit.

"We have to think things through," I told him. *"Running away is reacting, and we've done nothing wrong."*

"Tell that to the Coven."

His words knifed into my guts, hot, sharp, stabbing. I couldn't think about our former home. If I did, I'd burst into tears—or race back there and kill whoever showed up first. Eventually, they'd overpower me, toss me in their dungeon.

And never let me out. No judge. No jury. Coven law was incontrovertible.

No matter how satisfying revenge would be, it would get us exactly nowhere.

"We'll talk about it later." My tone was firm, but Zeke wasn't a dog. He thought for himself. I hadn't heard the end of any of this. Not by a longshot.

Moving briskly forward, I checked signs and hunted for vacancies. They weren't overly plentiful, but one beckoned. I knocked on one more door. Surely, there'd be a place I could trade labor for a roof over my head.

Carving out thinking time was essential to plot our next steps. I don't think well when I'm hungry and shivering.

"Come on in," someone yelled.

I glanced at Zeke. He stared back. I see right through the glamour I slather over him, but humans can't.

"You heard the man." I crooked a finger at the wolf and pushed the door open.

A tall, spare fellow in his fifties with brown eyes and a bald pate hurried into the entry hall and stopped dead. Jeans hung low on his hips. A plaid lumberman's jacket covered a stained T-shirt. Scuffed motorcycle boots rose to just below his knees.

I stood straighter, which brought me slightly above his six-foot height. The only truly odd thing about me is my mismatched eyes. One is dark, the other white, sort of like albino eyes except mine doesn't have a trace of pink.

He nodded once, curtly. "What can I do for you, missy?"

"I was hoping for lodging."

"I have space. It'll be fifty a night, cheapest place in town."

I cleared my throat. Unless I robbed a bank, something I could probably pull off with magic, I had nothing. The Coven paid for everything. When they'd shown me the door, I left with the clothes on my back. I'd asked about my things and been told nothing was mine. Everything belonged to them.

Yeah, the fucking Coven. Bitches all around.

The landlord got the picture and made shooing

motions with both hands. "This ain't no charity, lady. Move on out of here."

Not his first rodeo. Homelessness was a huge problem in every big city.

"I can work. Cook. Clean. Whatever's needed." I rocked from foot to foot, waiting. So far, I'd played fair, but this was my sixth apartment building. Screw fair. I sent subtle waves of compulsion across the space between us.

I was the best thing since sharp knives. He'd be a fool to send me packing.

The creases in his forehead smoothed. He actually half smiled. "How long were you thinking of staying?"

Breath swooshed from me in a quiet sigh. "Only a couple of nights, and then we'll be moving on."

He glanced at Zeke, who wagged his tail.

I swallowed a snort. The wolf knew when to lay it on thick.

"Is he housebroken?"

"Yes, of course," I replied.

"Will he chew things up?"

More tail wags.

"He's well behaved," I murmured with a vision of Zeke's jaws clamped around a vampire's neck racing through my mind.

"Can you sew?" the man asked.

The question came out of left field.

"Um, sure," I lied. How hard could it be?

"Come this way." He turned and shambled down a long hallway. The building was well past its prime with peeling wallpaper and dirty floors. He could have put me to work with a mop but apparently had something else in mind.

Two floors up, he led us to a tiny room with a sewing machine and stacks of clothes next to it. "May as well get started." He jerked a thumb at the linens and garments. "Dinner's in an hour. You'll sleep in this room too."

Before I could comment about the lack of a mattress, he was gone.

I shoved the door shut and removed my sodden outer garments, hanging them on hooks. My shirt and trousers were wet too, but at least they had a shot at drying in the warmish room. I pried off my boots, stripped off my soaked socks, and hung them next to everything else.

Zeke curled up in a corner and was asleep in seconds.

I perched on a bench in front of the sewing machine and stared at it. I've never used one of these contraptions. Luckily, it was threaded. I memorized the pattern in case I ran out of thread and had to duplicate it. Next, I hunted for the controls.

After botching seams on the first two items, I got better. A cunning second thread on a round thing sat beneath the sewing platform. It promptly ran out. A bit of digging in a drawer in the sewing table yielded the manual.

I fist pumped the air. The goddess hadn't deserted me.

These dogeared pages proved it. I wound new thread around the bobbin—all those pesky parts had names—and was back in business soon.

Sheesh, the man hadn't even asked my name. Maybe he didn't want to know. In addition to no money, I also lacked ID. I'd need to remedy that, but it wouldn't be easy without a birth certificate.

Even if I had one, no one would believe I'd been born hundreds of years before in the Old Country.

Sewing wasn't difficult. My mind wandered as I plowed through the ripped and torn items. If I'd known what the Coven was up to, I'd have prepared better. I needed a computer and a phone. A way to access the Internet.

The dark web to put a finer point on it. Surely, denizens of the underworld could set me up with a driver's license—never mind I can't drive—and a social security number.

Would I need anything further? A passport, maybe?

Not unless I wanted to leave the country. To do that would require money. Trading labor for a room and food was all fine and well, but I needed a real job, one that paid regularly.

A faint chuckle tickled my lips. I imagined filling out a job application, notably the skills section. Creative spell development and deployment were my forte. Sniffing out and slaying evil another. Mortals know about magic, but they prefer it on the big screen.

Not in their neighborhood.

I can type. Maybe someone would hire me as a secretary.

I can clean, but I hate it.

Soft snores issued from Zeke. He'd stretched out, back against the wall.

A brisk knock startled me. Zeke growled and shot to his feet. Before I could get up to open the door, a key turned in the lock. The man from earlier stood there, arms crossed over his chest, and surveyed my progress.

"That the stack that's done?" He pointed.

I nodded.

"Good. You're quick. Dinner is now. If you want to eat, you'd best get moving. First floor. Follow the food smells."

He was gone as quickly as he'd arrived, pulling the door closed behind him.

Zeke shook himself and pranced to the door, tail pluming. Food sounded grand to him. Familiars always shared food in the Coven.

I finished the seam I was working on, turned the machine off, and stood.

"Hate to break it to you," I told Zeke, "but you're probably not welcome in the dining room."

He lifted his upper lip, displaying impressive fangs. *"I can beg with the best of them,"* he informed me haughtily.

My clothes were mostly dry. I put my boots and stockings back on. Bringing Zeke wasn't the worst idea. I had no idea which winners of the world called this place home, but a large dog by my side would keep unwanted attention at bay.

"You're in," I told him.

He wagged his tail. His coat had dried and fluffed up around him, making him lusciously handsome. He has the same mismatched eyes as me. Of course, I cover them up with the glamour that makes him look like a dog.

Without belaboring the point, we dream our familiars and flesh them out with magic when our moon blood begins to flow. Mother was aghast when Zeke showed up sporting the same flaw she'd gone to the mat to conceal. She turned herself inside out casting spells to normalize his eyes.

It worked about as well as her efforts to fix me.

I opened the door and clucked at Zeke to follow me. We didn't need to be on the main floor to figure out where the dining room was. My senses are almost as acute as his. Following a food track was child's play.

Tonight's menu included a ground beef casserole with Mexican spices, stale corn tortillas, and tea. Hearty fare. The dining room was at the end of a lengthy hallway in the opposite direction from the front door. When we walked through, everyone fell silent, staring.

The landlord pushed to his feet and flapped a hand our way. "Let's welcome..."

Righto. He never did request my name.

"I'm Morgan." I nodded pleasantly at about thirty people, mostly men with a few women mixed in.

Everyone's face was marked by hard miles. There had to be stories here, but they weren't my affair.

"Yeah, let's welcome Morgan," he finished and stared at Zeke. "Don't recall inviting him."

Zeke whined and waved his tail around.

"He won't be any trouble," I promised. "He'll sit next to me and be a good boy."

A woof and more tail wags earned him a smattering of laughter. Before the landlord said, "No dogs," I crossed the room and helped myself to food from a table at the back. Plate and bowl in hand, I plopped into the nearest seat, put my head down, and inhaled the food.

It was the first meal I'd had since yesterday afternoon when the Coven handed us our walking papers, and I was hungry. Magic is a picky bitch of a mistress. No way to keep it in tip-top shape without adequate rest and nourishment.

I might not need my skills for a while, but it wasn't a reason to let them go to hell.

Mercifully, no one was in a chatty mood. Everyone hunkered over their food. Some returned for seconds until the serving dishes were empty. Hard times did that to you, made you not waste anything. Zeke hadn't gotten so much as a fat scrap.

He could slip out and hunt later. Or remain inside. Plenty of mice here. I sensed them in the walls and above the ceiling.

My sole experience with "hard times" was the last

twenty-four hours. Always been a quick learner, though. Some of my fellow tenants had already left. I bussed my dishes to a plastic bin in the back of the room with Zeke clinging to my side.

Living well is the best revenge. In my case, living at all was closer to the mark.

I racked my brain for who'd said that and came up with George Herbert. The Coven had an extensive library, filled with modern and ancient tomes. And we'd had the Internet. Many of the older witches made a sigil against evil when they passed the small study filled with CPUs and monitors, but we young ones lapped up the information.

If I was going to show the Coven I'd survive despite their crap, I needed a plan. Running away from Seattle wasn't part of it.

We walked out of the dining room. Zeke bounded the length of the hall to the front door. I opened it and let him out. He catapulted into darkness. The night was clear and cold. For once, the rain had let up.

"I'll let you know when I'm back," he woofed and vanished.

"Be careful. Don't let anyone see you."

He didn't answer. When he was beyond the reach of my glamour, he wrapped himself in invisibility.

I let the door shut and turned intent on trudging upstairs to our tiny room. With my belly full, I was sleepy.

"Aren't you going to wait for him?" An unfamiliar male voice jarred me.

I halted and turned, staring at the stairwell. One of my fellow diners stood at the bottom of the steps. Maybe mid-thirties, he had long, fair hair, a full beard, and the greenest eyes I'd ever seen. Faded Levis were cinched by a black leather belt. A wrinkled pale-blue shirt showcased broad shoulders, suggesting a well-muscled build.

How to respond? Responsible pet owners didn't abandon their charges.

I squirmed, hoping to project embarrassment. "I was just heading to the ladies'. He'll sit by the door and wait for me if he gets back first." To add credibility to my words, I started up the linoleum-coated steps.

The man loped up the stairs until he stood next to me. Damn, he was tall. It's rare when I have to look up—at anyone. My spine tingled unpleasantly. A warning?

My experience beyond the Coven's walls and orders is so limited I wasn't sure how to interpret the shudder. Better safe than sorry, though. I offered a curt nod. "Thank you for your concern about Zeke."

I placed a foot on the next step up.

He grabbed my forearm.

Panic swamped me. Crap. Would I have to fight my way out of this?

"Let go," I growled, doing a credible imitation of Zeke.

Unfamiliar power surged through where he held me. I

wrenched my arm to get away, but I may as well have been chained to a boulder.

His green gaze bored into mine. "Well, Morgan. Let's see what you've got."

I bristled, anger taking over. "Whatever I have isn't for you. Unhand me."

Laughter rolled from him. I hadn't expected it.

"Stop laughing at me."

He laughed harder—and hung on just as tight.

"I know what you are," slithered across my mind. *"Let's see what you've got was an invitation to see if you can escape."*

A red-hot poker up my ass wouldn't have been any more galvanizing. Heedless of consequences, I blasted through protections he'd erected around his magical center. It was absurdly simple. His eyes widened with shock at how quickly I'd laid waste to his defenses.

He let go of me and bowed. "I defer to superior talent."

My jaw hung open. I clacked it shut. "But you're—"

He clamped a hand over my mouth. "Un-uh."

"Let me in." Zeke howled.

Mr. No Name grinned. "Duty calls, eh."

"Yeah, he's not very patient."

Before the last of my words were out, I was alone. One moment, the Fae stood next to me; the next he was gone without a trace. No wonder he'd intercepted Zeke's mind speech.

Shaking my head, I trotted down the stairs to admit

the wolf. He was more than capable of opening the door by himself, but gratuitous displays of magic were frowned upon.

He pranced and danced in the lower hallway and then ran rings around me as we mounted the stairs. Back in our room, I draped a sound shield around us.

Zeke's ears pricked forward. *"Why the need for secrecy?"*

"We're not the only mages here," I informed him. "We've been outed."

CHAPTER TWO, DAMIEN

I've worked undercover for the Fae for the better part of the last two centuries. Or I did, until I quit. Used to be a much easier business. The primary part of my job was making certain we stayed two steps ahead of vampires and demons. Contrary to urban legends, our ability isn't especially strong.

Our Dark Fae cousins spin magical circles around us, but we're not going to talk about them. The other thing I did for my people was ensure an intact supply chain. Back when everyone lived an agrarian life, it was simple to divert a cow or a sheep.

Food sitting in refrigerated cases poses a far different problem. Stores have security guards. Farms and ranches have shifted from family operations to big conglomerates.

And now I'm whining.

I requested help, but our council wasn't forthcoming.

From their perspective, I'd never required assistance before, so they weren't inclined to offer it now.

They don't spend time beyond their cloistered halls. I've invited them to patrol with me. Never gotten any takers. Aye, big surprise. The human world is too gritty for their delicate sensibilities.

Faery shares a border with Earth, one marked by veils. The only ones who can pass are other Fae.

At least, that's the theory.

In practice, nearly anyone with a soupcon of magic can defeat our warding and enter Faery. It's caused untold problems, and they all fell on my head.

Sick of being underappreciated, I told the council to find another whipping boy and left. That was maybe twenty years ago. Or it might have been closer to thirty. Time is slippery when you live forever.

I talk big. In reality, I continued to keep an eye on our borders. No reason for my kinsmen to suffer a demon incursion. They'd be ill-prepared, and I didn't want the demise of my people to haunt me for the rest of my days. Because their backs were against the wall, they must have figured out the food problem without my intercession.

I've worked a few jobs, mostly construction. Every decade or so, I've had to move to a city where no one knows me, set up new fake ID, and establish myself all over again.

Seattle was my third home away from home. I've been here three years. Sometimes I grow lonely, but I'm too stubborn to go home. Besides, if I did, naught would change. I'd be shunted back into both my roles with nary a, "Grand to see you, Damien."

Nor a, "How've you been?" Or, "We've missed you."

Not much happens in my current life. Still, it's a refreshing change from constantly being on guard. I get up, go to work, collect a paycheck, and repeat the whole mess. My flat on Capitol Hill is basic, but the food is good. Earlier tonight, I nearly fell out of my chair when a witch and her familiar waltzed into the dining room.

It's not that mortals don't know about magic. They do. Most prefer to pretend it doesn't exist. Or is the purview of Hollywood. I've crossed paths with the occasional mage. We lift a stein or two and part company without swapping life stories.

No one cares. Not really.

I've also crossed paths with evil. Depending on which iteration of monster, I've either squashed them like bugs, or stayed out of their way. No point being an unsung hero. It's not as if I can call for backup.

I could picture how well that would go.

"Got yourself into this one, Damien."

"Aye, you should have known better."

"And you can damn well get yourself out."

I grimaced and glanced around at my humble chamber, the spot I'd vanished to after I left Morgan on the stairs. A narrow bed hugged the wall beneath one window. A sink and mirror sat in the corner. My few possessions were stashed in a closet. The only other item in the room was a desk. My laptop was locked in a drawer.

Back to the witch. I'd never actually seen one before tonight. From what I'd been taught, they never left their Covens. Had Morgan been ostracized? Did it have something to do with her odd eyes? The wolf masquerading as a dog had the same mismatched orbs.

I'd frightened her when I'd challenged her to break my hold. But she'd embarrassed the fuck out of me by wrenching free without breaking a sweat. Fae aren't exactly giants in the magical world.

I'm about as good as it gets.

Pathetic, huh? Witch enchantment shouldn't have overshadowed mine, but it did.

Whoever Morgan was, and whatever her story, she was a knockout with a tall, lithe build. Her tan cargo pants and blue stretchy top hadn't done much to hide shapely shoulders, rounded breasts, flared hips, a flat stomach, and long legs. Shiny dark hair spilled to mid-back level. Rings circled several fingers.

One eye was so dark, it was almost black. The other was white without a pupil. Was she blind in that eye? Had it been an accident? I pinched the bridge of my nose. Probably not. Or the wolf wouldn't have the same eye configuration.

Must be a magical thing, perhaps representative of their connection.

The wolf was gorgeous. Pure white and huge. He

probably weighed a good 150 pounds and had compelling eyes, one amber, one white like the witch's.

What were they doing here?

My curiosity was running full bore. I hadn't been this interested in anything since taking up residence in mortal-land.

After grabbing a towel, I walked down the hallway to the men's shower. Like I said, this place isn't fancy. Washroom facilities are shared, except for my sink. I got lucky there. Most of the rooms didn't have one.

As I cleaned up and readied myself for work tomorrow, I considered Morgan. She intrigued me. Had I spooked her enough to force her out of here?

It was a distinct possibility.

After returning to my room, I meandered back and forth. To reach out.

Or not.

What if she and the wolf were already gone?

I stretched faint tracking threads. Breath swooshed from me once I ascertained they were still in the building. Maybe this could wait until tomorrow. She'd just arrived.

Surely, she wouldn't leave so soon.

I wrapped a blue terry cloth robe around myself and sat on the edge of the bed to brush out my hair. The guys on the crew razz me about it, but Fae hair is sacred. I'll move to another place before I let anyone guilt me into cutting it.

My locked door blew open. Morgan and the wolf

stormed through. He was growling, fangs on full display. She kicked the door shut behind them and stomped in front of me.

"Why did you just check on me?" she demanded.

Oh-oh. "I tried to be, erm, subtle."

"Subtle like a freight train." She snorted.

"So long as you're here, have a seat." I patted the bed.

"On the bed, next to you? No thanks. Answer my question."

The wolf was still growling.

No way out of this one. Nothing simple. Summoning my feeble magic, I erected a sound shield around us. The walls in this building may as well have been made of paper mâché.

After a long, pointed glance, she tossed magic into the mix. Once the casting gelled, I said, "I've never seen a witch outside her Coven. You intrigue me."

"Is that all?" Arms crossed over her chest, she tapped a booted foot.

I softened my tone, added shades of safety and calm, and nodded. "If you're in trouble, have need of a friend, maybe I can—"

"I don't," she snapped.

The wolf woofed. *"We do too need help."*

His words were probably meant for Morgan, but I had no trouble hearing him.

"Keep your opinions to yourself," she told him.

"I can hear you both," I pointed out to keep everything on the up and up.

She curled her upper lip. "Forget you ever met us. We'll be gone soon enough."

Zeke had stopped growling, but he'd splayed the bulk of his body across the door. *"We had trouble finding this place."* The wolf's tone was even. *"He knows more about living here than we do."*

I drew my robe more tightly around me, cinching the sash. "Glad to help, but I can't if you don't tell me what you need."

Indecision sharpened her features. After a long moment, she shook her head. "Not taking any chances. Stay out of our business."

Twisting, she stomped to where Zeke barred the door. Something passed between them. This time, I couldn't make it out, but the wolf moved aside, and the pair left, shutting the door behind them.

The sound of footsteps and nails clacking on wood reached me through the door. Like I've said, no soundproofing here. My sound shield had gaping holes in it from the places Morgan had withdrawn her contribution. I reeled the rest of it in and traded my bathrobe for trousers, a shirt, a beat-up leather jacket, and ancient running shoes.

Dressed, I rocked from foot to foot, indecisive as fuck. I should reverse the process, remove my garments, and get into bed. It was nearly ten. Instead of following my own advice, I drew magic round me, shaped it into a teleport spell, and set my destination for Faery.

Weak magic or not, all Fae can zero in on our ancestral home. Doesn't even take that much in the way of enchantment to get there. My spell ran true, and the walls of our generational library rose around me, My needs must have preceded me; books and scrolls thumped onto the same oaken table where I'd learned the history of my people.

The large room with its floor-to-ceiling shelves was deserted. I'd expected as much. Scholarship has fallen out of fashion. No Fae have been born in over a century—not sure quite why. Those of us who were fully grown rarely took advantage of one of the richest troves of magical history in all the worlds: ours.

Not sure exactly what I sought, I dropped into a padded leather chair and dragged the nearest scroll in front of me.

Hours later, I was still reading. My knowledge about witches had expanded considerably. The only reason Morgan was running about loose had to be she'd been expelled from her Coven.

From what I'd read, no witch ever had told her Coven to pound sand and walked away.

Expulsion was a harsh move, one rarely exercised. Unlike Faery, witches had few rules and much latitude for pushing boundaries. I rolled my shoulders back and laced my fingers, cracking the knuckles. If Morgan had been ostracized for misbehavior, it was hard to imagine what it might have been.

If she'd raised magic against one of her sisters, they'd have imprisoned her deeming her too dangerous to be loose in the world.

And then there was Zeke. I hadn't known most witches had familiars. More surprising, very few were felines. So much for myths about witches and their black cats. I pulled one of the scrolls I'd read closer and unrolled it to the part about witches and their familiars to make sure I'd gotten it right.

According to whoever had penned this scroll, witches engaged in a ceremonial joining with their animals after their moon blood began to flow, but they met long before. The pairing began during infancy through trances and dreams. By the time the animal broke through from somewhere—the scroll was hazy about that part—the two already had a relationship.

Witches were always female. In olden times, they'd shanghaied likely men as sperm donors, killing them once they'd fathered a few children. Did they still do that? Unlikely. Much simpler to raid sperm banks today.

I still hadn't found what I sought, so I kept reading.

Finally, when dawn must be breaking on the Earth side of the veil, I stumbled across a reason Morgan and Zeke had turned into nomads. It had to be their eyes. Witches prided themselves on physical perfection.

Breath hissed from between my teeth. The only ones

who ever saw them were other Coven members. If the lore was to be believed, Covens didn't interact with other Covens. They were unique to themselves.

I glanced at my wrist from habit, but my smartwatch didn't work here.

I'd known it wouldn't. Nothing electronic operates in Faery. Even if devices could power on, there's no Internet or satellite connection.

After splaying my hands on the table, I pushed to my feet. I was stiff from sitting for so long, but I was armed with knowledge.

She'd told me to buzz off, but Zeke recognized me as an ally. Perhaps he'd prevail. If he did, I'd be more ready than I'd been a few hours ago.

On my way out of the library, a familiar voice hailed me. "Damien, what are you doing here?"

Crap. I did not want to get roped into a conversation that would make me late for work. Much like the Mer people, the Fae are constitutionally incapable of saying anything quickly.

"Nothing important," I shot back.

Before Logan, one of the council members, could catch up with me, I made a grab for the dregs of my teleport spell and got the hell out of Faery.

CHAPTER THREE, MORGAN

"Why wouldn't you let him help?" Zeke yipped once we were back inside our room.

"He's a stranger. Could have ulterior motives." I kept my voice low.

"He doesn't. We can trust him." The wolf's words held conviction.

"You have no way of knowing."

Hackles shot up the length of Zeke's spine.

Oh-oh. I'd hurt his feelings. I reached out to stroke him, but he shied away.

I perched on the stack of linens and garments I had yet to mend. "This is new for us both. We can't afford to make mistakes."

"Damien isn't a mistake," the wolf insisted.

"How do you know his name?" I asked.

"From his mind. He trusted me enough to let me in."

Fascinating. "What else did you find out?"

The hackles lowered a few notches, but Zeke kept his distance.

"He's Fae—"

"I knew that part," I broke in, but backed off fast after the wolf growled. "I'm sorry. Shouldn't have interrupted you."

"He's old. Used to work for his people, but he left. He's lived other places before coming here."

"Does that make him like us?" I mused. "A mage without a country."

Zeke shook his shaggy head. *"He left voluntarily. But don't you see? He found his way in a strange place. Means he might have resources we could use."*

I leaned against the wall. The wolf's instincts have always been sound. "You like him," I said.

A soft woof verified my impression.

"I'll look for him tomorrow."

Another woof was followed by a tail wag. No more hackles. Zeke padded next to me and lay down. I leaned against him.

My eyes fluttered shut. We'd spent the previous night huddled under a bridge with a few other homeless souls. I'd set wards, not trusting we'd be left alone, but it had been foolish. Even wearing a glamour that made him look like a cross between a brown lab and a Bernese Mountain dog, Zeke was still imposing.

Bothering a lone woman was one thing. A lone woman with a large dog, quite another.

I drifted in and out of consciousness as I turned over what to do next. At some point tomorrow, I'd run out of mending. Did it mean my tenure in this spot would end as well?

Wishing I knew more about rules in the mortal world, I went back to playing one scenario off against another. I'd been plenty conversant with Coven rules, and look where it had gotten me.

Fucking nowhere.

Should we remain here?

Another city, one without a resident witch population, might be a better bet. Or not. I'd run up against the same issues no matter where we went. My lack of basic job skills meant I'd end up in some dead-end, entry-level position, at the mercy of damn near everyone.

I have a shit ton of pride. It wouldn't take long for my temper to get the better of me. The moment I raised magic against anyone, I'd be screwed. Someone would call out the supernatural cop division. Every major city had one, if television shows were to be believed.

They'd chuck me into an ironclad cell, leaving Zeke to fend for himself. Not that he couldn't, but he does better when my glamour shields him. He'd have to make it from the center of the city to forest land. Remaining invisible for so long would drain his reserves.

I was still leaning against the wall. Slumping, I

wadded up the mending into an impromptu bed and curled next to Zeke. My mind was too busy to truly sleep. I missed my room in the Coven. On a top floor, I'd had a grand view of Seattle from upper Queen Anne Hill. My feather bed was soft; my furniture well-oiled teakwood.

Had another witch moved in already?

Fury vied with sorrow. Hecate's tits. I was such a sniveling wimp. The transition from "I'll show all of you," to a pity party was abrupt and unsettling.

Not to mention a waste of emotional energy.

Forward momentum was needed, not wallowing in a past that would never come back to life. Zeke snuggled closer. I draped an arm around his furry body, grateful for the pure, clean animal smell of him. The Coven had tried to hold onto him. They'd told him they'd use magic to reassign him to another witch. And fix his eyes.

Ha. If it were possible, Mother would have finessed it.

Zeke had lunged at Abigail, his fangs snapping inches from her throat.

She'd backed down quickly. Whoever had made a bid for Zeke would be disappointed, but engaging in a brawl with a 150 pound magical wolf wasn't worth it.

My eyes snapped open. Mother. She hadn't been there. Of course, she hadn't. If she were, she'd have stood up for me. Very few witches are fortunate enough to bear children. Each Coven has a lottery system. Every five years, the lead witch breaks into a sperm bank and makes off with the goods.

Everything is researched beforehand through the Dark Web, so she knows which vaults to steal from. I can't speak to how other Covens operate, but we were on a quota system. No more than three new witches every five years. As our ranks swelled, we formed sub Covens. Via a method I was never privy to, a few of us moved to other spots, but always as a group.

Would Mother try to find me?

I hoped not. Seeking me out would be forbidden. If she did, they'd never let her back inside. Bad enough one of us was an exile. An image of Zoelle with her flowing red tresses and eyes as green as Damien's filled my mind. She'd defied Coven rules by hiding my flawed face.

Awk. Damn it. Was she missing because they'd punished her? Something less severe than exile, but significant nonetheless.

The tears I'd struggled to contain followed. I was quiet about it. No reason to wake Zeke. I'd only mourn once. After tonight was done, so was I.

No more self-pity. No more shame. I'd done nothing wrong. I couldn't help my eyes. I was still me. If the Coven couldn't recognize it, I didn't want to be part of them.

Light streaming through my one window, and a staunch knock jolted me awake. "Best get back to that sewing," filtered through the thin door. "Breakfast's in half an hour."

"Thank you for letting me know," I called back and rolled to my feet.

"I want breakfast," Zeke announced from his spot on the floor.

"Me too. First, I'm going down the hall to the bathroom. Then I'll let you out, and we'll eat. Deal?"

He woofed an answer, and I got back into yesterday's clothes. They were all I had, a problem I'd need to remedy soon. I didn't have so much as a bathrobe to slink around in while I washed my garments.

They were starting to smell, so I doused them with a bit of clearing magic. It wasn't as effective as soap and water, but it would do for now.

I looked up and down the hall before striding toward the community bathrooms. One was labelled "Men," the other "Women." A glance inside shocked me. Mold peppered the walls and ceiling. I could almost see bacteria and viruses crawling up the walls. The tile floor was cracked. Three sinks, three toilets, and two showers offered no privacy at all. But I was the only one here, so what did it matter? Part of a broken mirror clung to the wall above the sinks. No one had cared enough to replace it.

I'd had my own bathroom in the Coven's guild house. At first, I hated to touch anything in this germ-riddled room, but witches never get sick. I could overlook a spot of grit and dirt. Maybe when I was done sewing, I'd pitch the landlord to keep me on as a housekeeper. The place certainly needed help.

Twenty minutes later, Zeke and I walked into the

dining room. He'd run outside long enough to relieve himself and tease the resident squirrel population. Just like last night, everyone kept to themselves. I got food, found an unoccupied table, and sat down.

The coffee was passable, the fare basic. Sausage, eggs, and toast. White toast with phony butter.

Shut up, diva, an inner voice hissed. *It's free, and we need to keep up our strength.*

I glanced around, seeking Damien, but he wasn't here. Had he eaten earlier? The landlord had indicated breakfast had only begun a few minutes ago, so either he wasn't here yet or he'd made other arrangements for the morning meal. After eating everything on my plate, I stood intending on seconds, but the serving dishes were empty.

Good lesson. Take as much as you need the first time around.

After dropping my dishes in the same plastic bin from the previous evening, I walked out of the dining room with Zeke at my heels.

The proprietor stood in front of me, barring my way. "Think you'll be done with that sewing today, missy?"

I almost bristled. Almost ordered him to use my given name. Instead, I kept my gaze downcast and nodded.

"If you plan to stay on afterward, you'll have to pay, same as everyone else," he informed me and stalked off. Like me, he wore yesterday's clothes except his smelled worse than mine.

"Hungry," Zeke complained.

Of course, he would be.

"We'll take care of that," I reassured him, "but we'll do it from the room. Not from here."

I locked the door behind us and set a journey casting to take us to lush, rolling hills north of the city. We'd hunted there when we lived in the Coven's guild house. No reason not to use this meadow. I'd occasionally run into other witches here. If we did, we'd cross that bridge when it showed up.

They'd kicked me out of the Coven, not out of the world.

Time slid past while Zeke hunted, ate, and located more prey. Wolves can get by with infrequent meals since they gorge themselves. So far, no one roamed the forest except us—and Zeke's food.

I wandered through thick undergrowth and ancient stands of trees, soothed by their song. I was still a witch, damn it. My power was intact. The Coven had robbed me of my home and sisterhood, but they hadn't taken my pride or skill.

"Morgan," floated on the air.

My head snapped around as I sought the source. Nothing popped out, so I tossed magic in an arc. It returned emptyhanded. I stopped in the center of half a dozen evergreen trees.

"Who's there?"

"Since when don't you recognize my voice?"

Despite my brave words from the night before, my eyes flooded. "Mother? Where are you?"

"Not there, so you can stop looking." Her words held a note of asperity I remembered all too well.

"But where, then?" I pressed and girded myself for her reply.

"I figured if I waited, you and Zeke would come along. This is the nearest hunting ground to the city. Good to see you well, Daughter. I am sorry I could not intervene."

I choked on a sob, still searching for her. "Where are you?"

"They didn't hurt me. I am all right. It's all you need to know."

I murmured, "I love you," and brushed tears off my cheeks.

"I will always love you, daughter of my heart. Believe in yourself, Morgan. You are stronger than you realize. Resources will come to you. Your eyes are not why they kicked you out of the Coven. Not the real reason, although some will insist they are."

Shock spilled through me. "If not them, then what?"

Zoelle didn't answer. When I searched for her essence, she was gone.

Zeke bounded up, chewing the remains of something. "Is there time for one more?"

I checked my internal clock and sucked in a breath. "No. We should have left an hour ago."

I resurrected my spell, hoping against hope we could

sneak into the boardinghouse unnoticed. It could work if the damned proprietor hadn't knocked on my door to check on me.

The return journey was uneventful. Zeke took up his spot beneath the window, and I pulled a ripped sheet into my arms. The sewing machine had no sooner began to buzz when my door flew open.

The landlord stomped into the room. His bushy gray eyebrows were drawn into a thick, disapproving line. He stabbed a finger my way. "Is this how you repay generosity, missy? I've been looking for you, and up until right now, you weren't here. I didn't see you walk through the front door.

"What the hell? Are you one of those creatures? Did you fly in here on a broomstick?"

Zeke woofed pleasantly, tail wagging, as if to offer a calm oasis of doggie love.

I should have stopped myself, but I burst out laughing.

"What's so blasted funny?" the man demanded, his face blotching an angry red.

I kept on sewing to hopefully prove my usefulness. "That you think I'm a witch or something," I managed between giggles.

"How'd you get in here?" He crossed his arms over his chest. "Been watching the front door once I knew you wasn't here."

I thought fast, building a mental map of the building.

"We took the fire escape." I offered a disingenuous smile. "Then I stopped in the bathroom since the fire escape door's right next to it. Then we came here. I'm sorry we were gone so long. Zeke was having a good time. I promise I'll get all this mending done before dinnertime."

"Fire escape?" Incredulity sharpened his tone. "No one uses it."

"We just did. Was it wrong? Is there some rule against it?"

The sheet was done. I folded it and extracted the next item in the stack, smoothing it to determine what needed stitching.

Zeke padded to the man and rubbed against him. He can be charming, and pushy. In this instance, he served as a distraction.

"Why should I believe you?" the man demanded, but he did scratch Zeke's head. The wolf leaned into his touch.

I'd positioned a length of curtain under my presser foot, but I looked up. "Because none of the other explanations make any sense. If I was a witch, or something magical who could fly into this room, why would I even be here? Don't all those paranormal people have scads of cash?"

"Mmph. Good point. Fine. I'm leaving. See that you finish everything."

"I promised, didn't I?" Before he turned to leave, I

tossed out, "Any chance I could trade cleaning for a few more nights?" I followed my suggestion with a smidge of coercion, so he'd view my idea as the best thing since automobiles were invented.

"I'll think about it," he mumbled and shuffled out of the room. Zeke tugged the door shut by closing his jaws around the knob.

"That was close," the wolf observed. *"How'd you know about the fire escape?"*

"Caught a glimpse of it before we came inside last night."

"I see."

He retreated to the window and curled in a ball. I worked my way through the torn items, my mind busy.

I'd bought us a little time, emphasis on a little. The landlord would never let me stay more than a handful of days. While I worked here, I couldn't very well be earning money elsewhere—if anyone would even hire me.

The same clump of problems from yesterday hadn't gone anywhere. Without ID, there'd be no job. I might muscle my way in with magic, but unless I was being paid under the table, someone would need a social security number and probably picture ID.

Items I lacked.

Having Mother seek me out both warmed and worried me. She'd known where to find me, which meant others in the Coven would too. We'd have to locate another spot for Zeke to hunt, but it wouldn't be necessary for a couple of days. I hadn't told him about her visitation—or whatever it had been—and I needed to.

What she'd said gnawed at the edges of my mind. If not my eyes, then why had I been considered such a threat they had to rid themselves of me? Furthermore, why did Mother know, and I didn't?

The Coven had layers of self-government, something I'd never been interested in. If Mother had known something was up, why hadn't she warned me?

My mind flashed back to when I'd last seen her; it was several months ago. I'd thought her absence odd, but now it made sense. The elders had placed her where she couldn't alert me.

For all I knew, she'd been working to break through this entire time.

A knock was followed by, "Dinner in fifteen." For once, the landlord's voice was friendly. Perhaps he'd rethought his suspicions about me.

I only had two items left to mend. I'd finish them after dinner. No point working myself out of a job before bedtime.

On my feet, I finger combed tangles out of my hair.

Zeke bounded to his feet and ran to the door, tail wagging madly. I didn't have to guess to know who was on the far side.

Sure enough, a knock was followed by the knob turning and Damien's beefy form standing in the doorway. "Coming to dinner?" he asked, a broad smile on his face. In addition to green eyes, he had a high forehead, square chin, and artistic cheekbones. But then, the Fae always were lovely. A glamour smoothed the points of his ears.

"I was planning on it," I replied.

"Care to accompany me?"

Zeke woofed a yes for us both, and we followed Damien into the hallway. I tugged the door shut and sealed it with a quick spell in case the nosy landlord chose the dinner hour to do a bit of prying.

Back when he'd been convinced I was a sorceress, he'd unlocked my door and peered within. If he'd come inside, I'd have sensed it. I'd put the kibosh on his supernatural theory, which meant he might be more inclined to snoop since he wasn't afraid of paranormal retribution.

"Where were you at breakfast?" I asked Damien.

A grin split his chiseled lips. "I'll take it as a good sign you noticed I wasn't there."

"Overslept?" I shot a sidelong glance his way.

He shook his head. "I work construction. We start hella early."

I nodded, absorbing the information. He had a job. Meant he had ID. Zeke was convinced we could trust him.

I was moving closer to deleting a few bricks from my wall. I didn't used to be this cautious. Being expelled from the Coven had rattled my equanimity and shot holes in the trusting attitude I typically led with.

"What are you building?" I asked.

We walked into the dining room. "I'll tell you over supper," he promised and patted a table. "This one all right?"

"Sure."

He plopped into a chair. "Go fill a plate. Once you're back, I'll do the same."

It's not my nature to obey blindly, but in this instance, I hustled to the food table and took a generous portion of beef stew, sliced tomatoes, and stale bread with the same disgusting fake butter from breakfast.

Zeke remained with Damien. Interesting. First time he'd left my side other than when he hunted.

Mother had intimated fortune would find me. Was Damien its leading edge? Time would tell. Too bad I didn't have the luxury of waiting things out. I'd have to make a move one way or another long before I could be certain of the Fae's intentions.

Meant I'd have to trust him—or not—and figure out which horse I'd be betting on soon.

CHAPTER FOUR, DAMIEN

I'd hesitated before presenting myself at Morgan's door, but rejection doesn't faze me. Worst she could have done was tell me to get lost.

She hadn't.

After she returned with a healthy portion of tonight's fare, I filled my plate and sat across from her. One of the things I appreciate about this boardinghouse is the residents mind their own affairs. Other than a pleasant nod, no one had even gone so far as to ask my name.

I'd done enough skulking through minds to know why. Nearly everyone here was hiding from something. Many used assumed names. Despite his slipshod appearance, the landlord ran a tight ship. He booted people who so much as smelled of trouble before they could cause problems.

Zeke positioned himself beneath the table where I

could pass him chunks of meat without anyone noticing. There was always enough food, barely. No leftovers ever made their way back to the kitchens. Judging from Morgan's plate, she'd learned that lesson this morning.

I glanced sidelong at her, grateful she was intent on finishing her food. Surely, food at the Coven had been more sophisticated.

She must have felt my gaze on her because she looked up. "You were going to tell me what you're building."

"So I was." I set my fork across my plate. "We're working on an apartment building in West Seattle. It'll be done soon, but the company I work for has projects on the books to take them well into next year."

"Must be nice," she murmured. "I need a job."

"What can you do?" I resumed eating again.

She grinned. It lightened the shadows behind her eyes. "Apparently, I wield a mean sewing machine. Beyond that, I can learn almost anything."

I considered how to phrase my next question. "What did you do at your last residence?"

The smile faded. "Nothing mortals would value." She bit her lower lip; her gaze skuttled around the room. No one sat very close to us, but it paid to be cautious.

"Hang on," I murmured and slopped a sound shield around us. It was different in that people would hear our voices, but the words would be altered to banal conversation. If anyone were listening, they'd think we were morons, but I didn't care.

She probed at the weave; a corner of her mouth twitched. "Creative," she mumbled around a mouthful of stew.

"Why thank you. I consider that high praise from someone whose talent outshines mine."

"Don't be so sure about that. Never would have occurred to me to insert those alterations into a sound shield."

I drained half my water glass, missing a good aged mead. Zeke licked my hand. "Sorry, mate," I told him. "All gone."

Morgan craned her neck to get a better view of her wolf. "You shouldn't beg," she admonished.

"Wasn't. He fed me of his own free will."

I snorted. "Does it mean he can compel handouts?"

Morgan nodded. Color rose to her pale cheeks.

"Feel like telling me what happened?" I reached across the table and patted her hand.

She shook her head.

"Why? You need to trust someone."

"Zeke said much the same, but I'm not ready. Can't afford to make mistakes."

Hmmm. Whatever had happened to her was still too new and too raw to sort through. "How long have you been, erm, free?"

Her cheeks reddened further. "Since afternoon two days ago."

Whoa. I'd guessed right. No wonder she was so reticent.

I blew out a measured breath. "I've never met a witch before. From what I know—and I spent most of last night in Faery's library researching your people—"

"You did? Why?" she broke in. Shock furrowed her forehead and formed lines at the corners of her eyes.

"Because I needed information. Whatever I knew about witches faded from memory centuries ago. You tend to keep to yourselves." I held my tone neutral. She was strung so tight, it wouldn't take much for her to jump up and run into the night.

"Last call for dishes," rang through the room. This wasn't elegant dining. They wanted to clear up and close the kitchen for the night.

I gathered our plates, silverware, and glasses, and carted them to a bin on the end of the serving table. When I returned to our table, Morgan was still there.

"Feel like a stroll?" I offered an arm. "We can continue our conversation."

She'd folded her hands in front of her on the table, gaze glued to her knuckles.

"*I want to go for a walk,*" Zeke announced. I offered silent thanks to my new ally.

Morgan pushed her chair away from the table and stood. She still wasn't looking at me as she led the way out of the dining room with Zeke at her heels. I brought up the rear.

"Do you want a coat?" I asked.

She shook her head. I held the front door open for her and the wolf and followed them through. The night was cold and damp, but it wasn't raining. I considered draping an arm around her shoulders, but didn't.

"Why did me reading about witches upset you?" I asked, genuinely wanting to know.

A shudder wracked her lanky frame. "Not sure," she mumbled. "It's almost like you were snooping."

"Aye, I was snooping. Because I care."

She stopped dead. Zeke was romping in a nearby thicket. He wore his customary glamour.

"Why would you care? You scarcely know me?"

I moved in front of her and dropped both hands on her shoulders. "True, but witches never leave their Covens. Yet, here you are with your familiar. You must have parted company with the sisterhood."

I held up a hand. "You needn't tell me why, but any mage newly arrived in a potentially hostile environment needs assistance. If you spent all your years in a Coven guild house, you know next to nothing about how to survive outside one."

She finally looked at me with her odd eyes. They were pinched at the corners, and the skin between her dark brows was furrowed. "Guess you've got my number. Everything I know about humans comes from TV and the Internet."

Shock spilled through me. "Electronics work inside a Coven guild house?"

Morgan nodded. "Why wouldn't they?"

"Because they're deader than doornails in Faery and every other magical land."

"Good to know," she mumbled.

We commenced walking again. A park was at the end of the next block. It was as good a place as any for Zeke to explore. Seattle has a leash law; I'd craft a magical one if we needed it.

When she didn't appear inclined to offer anything further, I went on, "Smyth hired you to do what? And for how long?"

Her head snapped toward me. "Who's— Never mind. Must be the proprietor. Yeah, he hired me to do a bunch of sewing, but I'm nearly done. I asked if he'd keep me on to clean. He's thinking about it."

"He's so tight, he squeaks," I murmured. "Even if he relents and gives you a couple of days, you'll need a real job eventually."

"Don't you think I realize that?" She stomped away from me, her boots squelching in the wet grass.

I ran to catch up. "Do you have identification? A driver's license? For that matter, do you know how to drive a car?"

"No, no, and no."

"All right. First things first. You need identification. No one will hire you for a real job without it."

She'd stopped again, this time beneath a large white fir tree. Water dripped from its branches and ran down her face. She faced me squarely, standing tall. "I also lack money."

I blinked a couple of times. What a callous bunch of bitches to send one of their own into the world so wretchedly unprepared.

"I could—" I began.

She waved me to silence. "I am not taking your money. I can make myself invisible and steal what I need. Until I get my feet under me."

"Bad idea."

"Why?"

"If anyone sees you, they'll alert the PDA."

"Huh? The what?" Her breath frosted the night air.

"Paranormal Detective Agency. It's a branch of the Seattle Police."

She chewed her lower lip. "Yeah, I know about those, but didn't know its name here locally. Fine. Zeke and I can go to, erm, Olympia or Yakima. Or some small town in Arizona. It doesn't rain there."

"PDAs are in all those places too," I informed her. "Mortals are not fond of us. So long as we abide by their rules and aren't in their face with spells, we're tolerated. But if you steal from someone, and they can't see who robbed them, they'll call 911."

"Whoa. There are that many cops, huh? Still can't see where it's a problem if I lay low," she muttered.

"The PDA is made up of mages," I explained. "They'll figure out quick enough who was responsible, and they'll find you with tracking spells."

"Oh." Her shoulder slumped.

Since her defenses seemed to be crumbling, I took a chance. "Why'd you leave the Coven."

"Not by choice, and it's all I'll say about it."

Interesting. My first guess that they'd kicked her out was spot on. What had she done? I hearkened back to my previous evening's research. The Fae library doesn't exactly contain the final word about other mages, but the scrolls I'd read had been quite clear only a capital crime merited expulsion."

"You don't look like an axe murderer." I focused my gaze on her.

She flinched. "I'm not."

Zeke loped over. *"Morgan is innocent. They didn't like our eyes. It's the only reason."*

She swatted at him. "Silence."

"Damien is on our side," he protested.

"I don't understand," I murmured. "Presumably, your eyes haven't changed. Why'd they wait until now to—"

"I released my habitual glamour." She tossed her head. "Took them less than a day to kick us out. Except they wanted to keep Zeke."

"I'd have torn out her throat," the wolf growled.

No wonder the head witch hadn't pressed it. I'd think

twice about tangling with Zeke in his true form. Anyone would.

"How much does ID cost?" Morgan glanced my way.

Her question came out of left field—or perhaps not. "Depends," I replied. "A basic set with a birth certificate and driver's license is around $2000. Adding a passport or high school diploma costs more."

Morgan's eyes widened. It probably sounded like a lot of money to her. "H-how do they do it?"

"They find someone about your age and appearance who's dead and borrow their identity."

"And that works?"

"Not always. Sometimes you have to start over. Depends how quiet a life the person led."

"I see."

Zeke stood next to her. She buried a hand in his fur. The two of them, soldiers against the world, touched me. "I wish you'd let me help. It would only be a loan. You could pay me back."

"I'd mean to, but what if I couldn't?" Wet from tree drippings, her hair clung to her head.

"That would be all right. Unlike your situation, the Fae have continued to underwrite me despite me leaving Faery. I work because I like to be busy, not because I need the money."

"Okay, but they wouldn't think much about you using their resources to support a witch and her familiar."

It was true, but no one ever asked where my funds went; neither were they likely to.

"Why do you stay?" she asked softly.

It took me a moment to understand she was asking why I had remained living among mortals. I guided us to a bench that wasn't positioned beneath dripping branches. It was still wet, so I set magic to dry it before sitting and patting the spot next to me.

After a pause, she sat about half a meter away.

I cleared my throat as I sought where to begin. "This isn't my first stint living among mortals," I began. "My work for my people included watching our portals to ensure nothing evil crossed into our lands. The other thing I did was procure food and transport it into Faery."

"You don't grow your own crops?" Her dark brows shot up.

"Some, but our land isn't all that fertile."

"Why'd you stop?"

It was the question of the hour, and one I'd asked myself many a time. "I wasn't appreciated. The Fae took my efforts for granted. No one ever offered to help. One day, I'd had enough. Since I was already living among mankind, it wasn't a quantum leap."

"Do you have regrets?" Her words were gentle, her voice low and musical.

"Sure. I still keep an eye on a few key border points. For years, I expected our council would replace me. When it became obvious they weren't going to, I reinstituted part of my patrol."

She clasped her hands in her lap and turned toward me. "You can still go back and forth?"

I nodded. "Aye, I'm still welcome in Faery."

She looked down. Long lashes grazed her cheeks. "Of course. Otherwise, how could you have studied all those library materials about the sisterhood. The Coven had an extensive library. I'm sure I'll miss it."

"It's a big change," I ventured.

"You have no idea. Or maybe you do. I'm still reeling, but I'll work things out. I have to, for Zeke and me."

He woofed softly and licked her arm.

"Ready to head back?" I asked.

She shivered. "Yeah. I'm cold. Should have brought my coat. I need clothes, among other things. These"—she swept a hand down her body—"are all I have."

Anger curled my guts into a knot. How could the Coven have shut her out with only the garments on her back? No money. No resources. It was criminal. Mages have ethical codes. Were witch protocols totally lacking in decency?

I stood and offered her a hand. To my surprise, she took it. Her fingers were like icicles, so I wrapped mine around them. Zeke trotted next to us as we retraced our steps to the boardinghouse.

Before we got there, she blurted, "Mother showed up when I took Zeke hunting today."

"What?" the wolf yipped. *"Why didn't you tell me? Why couldn't I sense her?"*

"Because all of her wasn't there," Morgan explained. "It was more like a sending."

"She must be worried," I ventured and stopped walking. The steps into our building were only a few feet away.

"I'm worried about her," Morgan murmured. "The Coven is punishing her, except I don't know how or even where she is. She wasn't at my excommunication hearing, and nothing could have kept her away."

"Except force or imprisonment," I tossed out, worried about her too.

"Exactly," Morgan agreed.

"What'd she say?" Zeke demanded.

"That it's not our eyes. They're not the reason for what happened. Only an excuse to force everyone to go along with whoever the ringleaders are."

I absorbed that bombshell. Someone must know something about Morgan, a key bit of information that had turned the others against her. I needed to do more sleuthing. Jump on this and follow it to its end. My network of spies was still mostly active. I'd begin there.

"We're not going to solve anything tonight." I added a touch of calm to my words.

With her wet hair, creased forehead, and slumped shoulders, she looked distraught. I guided her and Zeke inside and up the stairs to their room.

"Try and get a decent night's rest," I told them.

"You too." Morgan touched my hand. "You've lost enough sleep on my account."

I brushed my lips over her cheek, shocked by how cold her skin still was, and waited until they went inside and I heard the snick of the lock.

My research last night was only a beginning. Tonight, I'd tap my old sources to see if anyone knew something or could point me in a fertile direction.

Morgan was ambivalent about my help.

Too bad. She was getting it whether she wanted it or not.

I can be a stubborn bastard, and every protective bone in my body had been activated. I'd see no harm came to her. Zeke hadn't come out and said it, but I felt certain he'd welcome assistance in that regard. While I was at it, I'd do my damnedest to rain destruction on the Coven, who'd been shortsighted enough to exile her.

Walk away while you still can, a stern inner voice ordered.

I recognized that voice. It sounded suspiciously like one of my uncles. I'd internalized a lot of his wisdom. All mages are insular; we stick to our own kind. If my plan played out, I'd alienate every witch in the U.S. and beyond by meddling in their internal affairs. It would reflect unfavorably on the Fae.

I didn't care.

I hadn't been this revved up about anything since the

vampire wars back in the 1500s. I'm no Sir Galahad, but my personal damsel in distress lay on the far side of the door across the hall from me.

No more time to waste. I trotted toward the community bathroom intending to launch a travel spell from there.

CHAPTER FIVE, MORGAN

The sound of Damien's footsteps faded as he walked away. I blew out a shuddery breath and swathed myself in a couple of sheets to warm up. No bed meant no blankets. Nothing to cozy up in. Zeke sensed my discomfort and pressed against me, offering his body heat. I sat on my favorite stack of mended fabric and wrapped an arm around him.

I'd wanted to invite Damien into my room. For all the wrong reasons. He'd been kind to me, and I was still so raw from my treatment at the hands of my kinswomen, I craved comfort.

Kind was the operative term. He'd listened and cared enough to find out more about witches. Had he done it because of me specifically? Or because of an intellectual curiosity about another iteration of mage.

I squeezed my eyes shut. In addition to lacking ID and

practical job skills, I also knew less than nothing about men. He might have misinterpreted my motives if I'd asked him to join me in my room. I already mentioned the sperm bank. It's how we reproduce. We're supposed to remain celibate.

Rumors were always floating around about this witch or that slipping into dangerous territory by opening her legs for a comely man. Of course, no one would ever admit to such a fall from grace. In my years with the sisterhood, I'd never caught wind of an unauthorized pregnancy.

But then, I wouldn't have. We're witches. We have ways of dealing with such things.

My confusion about Damien unsettled me. So did unfamiliar longings that made me squirm. Sorting through them took so much effort, I pushed everything to a distant back burner.

"Told you he was one of the good ones." Zeke leaned into me.

I scratched between his furry ears. "Turns out you were right, dear heart."

"I usually am."

I elbowed him. "No modesty in your house."

"Why should there be?"

Good point. I was a little warmer, so I shed the sheets, got to my feet, and scanned my workspace. The landlord hadn't said boo since accusing me of nefarious magical ability. I'd sort of expected something, like a note with instructions—or orders to vacate his premises—but there was nothing of the kind.

Eh, no news was good news. Either he was still thinking about hiring me to clean, or he'd already decided I was a good bet. I chose to look on the bright side. If he was going to turn me out on my ear, he'd have written a note or changed the lock on the door or something.

Not that it would have been much of a deterrent. I can open any lock, and doing so didn't prove I possessed magic. A simple pickpocket could do much the same. Regardless, it hadn't been needed. The key in my pocket still turned the tumblers.

I snatched a mended towel and walked to the door.

"Where are you going?" Zeke's ears pricked forward.

"To the bathroom to wash my face."

He curled into a ball, tail tucked around him.

I clomped down the hall, trying not to make noise with my boots. Wetting a bit of towel, I wiped sweat and grime off my face. I'd have liked to brush my teeth, but I lacked a toothbrush. In lieu of bristles, I used a finger and water.

All the while, Damien's fair good looks hovered behind my eyes. I'd always imagined Fae to be slightly built, almost waiflike. He was broad and burly, so full of life it exploded around him.

I stared at my reflection in the glass and shook a finger at it. I had plenty to worry about. He was a complication I did not need. Besides, after I left this place—and leave I would sooner rather than later—I'd probably never see him again.

It was for the best.

Another woman who was in her fifties, give or take, wandered in. I smelled alcohol from ten paces, the telltale stench when someone metabolizes the stuff through their skin because they drink so much. We'd had a few witches like that.

She avoided eye contact and vanished into a toilet stall. I retraced my steps down the hall to my hovel of a room. Zeke uncurled his tail long enough to wag it a couple of times.

I shut and locked the door.

Tonight, I did a better job piling up the mending to make a pallet. A shot of magic killed the overhead light. Zeke snored softly. I closed my eyes, but sleep was a joke. Not because I wasn't tired, but because worry dogged me.

I'd have to make major decisions soon. Like, would we remain in this city?

"Fuck that," I muttered. "Am I going to confront the Coven, get to the bottom of why they kicked me out?"

"You have to," Zeke woofed.

So much for him being dead to the world.

"I don't have to do anything."

"You won't rest until you find out what's really going on," my wolf said.

He knows me better than anyone except maybe Mother—

My thoughts stuttered to a halt. Mother. To hell with

what had happened to me. We needed to locate her, free her if need be. It jumped to the top of my priority list.

Should I ask Damien for help?

Nope. I squelched that line of thought in its infancy. No way would I get him involved with the Coven. It could start a devastating war between witches and Fae. Not that mages don't fight one another, but it's always good against evil. In this instance, witches and Fae both work the good side of the street. Not exactly allies, but far from enemies.

I'd be damned if I'd drive a wedge between our two peoples on my behalf.

It left me where I'd begun: figuring this out on my own. After tossing a mental ball this way and that, I came up with a rough plan. Nothing would happen quickly. I'd have to do this in stages. First off, I would tap Damien to help me procure ID. Once I had that, I'd find work and save up some money.

It would take months before I was in a position to return to the Coven and confront the council. By then, they'd have mostly forgotten about me, which would work in my favor.

I hoped.

The simplest approach would be to remain in Seattle. At least I was familiar with this city. If the Coven had wanted me out of commission, they'd have consigned me to ancient dungeons deep in the Old Country.

If they truly existed. I'd never been certain, but we'd

all been raised on threats of being sent there if we didn't follow the rules. I muffled a snort and rolled over. Despite a few layers of cotton, the floorboards poked my hips.

Back when I was young, my Coven's home had been in the hills of northern England. No dungeons there, but an ancient castle several kilometers north of Carlisle housed part of my Coven. I'd visited but never made it past the first floor sitting room. The dungeons in the basement were off limits.

We'd come to the Americas during my first fifty years. Magic only goes so far, and even we can't teleport across oceans. Odd since we can leave Earth for contiguous worlds. Regardless, we'd commissioned a vessel and spent six storm-tossed weeks crossing the Atlantic.

The captain and his crew figured out soon enough we weren't a passel of loose women heading for Old West brothels when they tried to push themselves on us. After that failed, there'd been talk of returning to port or tossing us overboard.

We made short work of both by binding the captain to our will with magic. His crew fell into line. Good thing since a series of Hell-spawned storms threatened to capsize our puny craft.

When I look at modern ships, it amazes me those old buckets of bolts crossed a pond, much less an ocean.

I flopped onto my stomach, cradling my head in my arms. My thoughts were truly wandering. From dungeons to our early guild house on the outskirts of Carlisle to our long-ago ocean voyage. The Coven had been much smaller in those days. Even adding three witches every five years—and we'd done it the old-fashioned way before sperm banks, shanghaiing a likely man—had swelled our ranks since most of us are immortal.

The odd witch had flawed genetics and succumbed to old age, but not enough to balance our numbers. Moving beyond using men to provide for our needs had been a relief since none of them left the guild house alive. We couldn't afford the tales they'd tell.

My eyelids finally felt heavy. When I shut them, I dozed off and on. Zeke snuggled closer. The next day, I'd hunt for the landlord before breakfast to tell him I'd finished the mending and ask what he wanted me to work on next. If he didn't hand me my walking papers—and I did have some control over that—I'd seek out Damien at dinner and have him point me toward a place I could procure ID.

The $2000 was a stumbling block—a pretty damned big one—but I'd figure something out. Maybe whoever made the ID would be willing to trade for a spell or a charm. I can be convincing when the occasion arises. Not all mortals are averse to magic. Perhaps the shadier ones would be more intrigued by what I could bring to the table.

I must have finally drifted off since loud pounding on my door jolted me to a sit about the same time it slammed against the stops. The landlord stomped in.

"Not an early riser, eh?" He stared hard at me.

I hastily pulled the sides of my top together and murmured, "Sorry. Didn't sleep well."

"You must be used to fancier accommodations." Laughter spurted from him but stopped abruptly. "You done with the sewing, missy?"

My mind was still covered by a layer of fuzz.

Zeke sprang to his feet, shook himself, and ambled over to Smythe, tail swooshing this way and that. The wolf can be ingratiating, and Smythe scratched between his ears.

I started to get up, but I was half naked. Better to remain where I was. "I'm nearly done," I told him. "Only two pieces left. I'd planned to finish them before breakfast."

"Finish 'em after," he barked. "Kitchen staff's short today. Get on down there and help them."

He left as abruptly as he'd shown up. I dove into my clothes. They smelled worse each day, but I didn't have anything else to change into. And no one here smelled all that fresh—except Damien. His scent reminded me of rolling oceans and damp pine trees.

I grinned ruefully. He was never far from my thoughts. I'd have to establish better distance, but I didn't have to do it right this minute.

Zeke plopped his butt on the ground. *"Just like that,"* he woofed.

"Just like what?"

"Looks as if he hired you."

"Mmph. Guess he did, except I'm more like an indentured servant."

"What's that?" The wolf cocked his head to one side.

"Someone who works but isn't paid except in room and board. You have to stay here."

"Why?" Another tail swoosh.

"Because I bet they don't allow dogs in the kitchen. I'll come back for you when it's breakfast time."

"But I want to go outside."

Breath rattled from me. "Stay out of sight. Do not draw attention to yourself. And don't go so far my glamour fades and reveals what you are."

The wolf made a chuffing sound, the lupine equivalent of laughter. *"Yes, Mother."*

I stroked his head and hurried from the room.

The kitchen staff turned out to be one harried middle-aged man wearing a stained white apron. At the moment, he was stirring pots on an industrial-sized stove. About six feet tall, he had a paunch and a mostly bald head. Rheumy blue eyes had more than a few miles on them.

"Where's everyone else?" I asked.

He laughed. "That's rich. You the broad Smythe scared up?"

Resentment simmered. I beat it back. "That would be me," I agreed cheerily.

"Fine. Get chopping." He pointed at a stack of moldy potatoes on a board.

"How big?" I asked and wielded a knife that proved to be duller than dirt. I fixed it with a swipe of magic.

His eyes might have widened for a moment; or I could have imagined it."Up to you. Surprise me," he replied.

I didn't ask his name. He didn't ask mine. When I had a few potatoes cubed, he tossed them in hot oil. Once I was done with the potatoes, he sent me out to stack dishes on the sideboard.

All in all, he was easy to work with. Maybe I'd overestimated the difficulty of living in a world filled with humans.

People were filtering into the dining room a few minutes before breakfast time. For once, they chattered animatedly. I listened as I ferried dishes and silver, catching snatches of an event that was unfolding a few blocks away.

At first, I didn't pay close attention—until someone mentioned a white wolf. The stack of plates in my arms almost crashed to the floor. If I hadn't swooped in with magic, I'd have been standing ankle deep in shards.

I should have ducked into the kitchen, told the dude stirring pots I had to run out for a few. Instead, I scuttled out the door, ran down the hallway threading my way between people heading for breakfast, and burst through the front door.

A quick surge of magic showed me where to find Zeke.

Crappity crap. Why couldn't he have done what I told

him and stayed close to home? Or at least turned invisible before trouble struck.

Magic at the ready, I pelted forward. I'd fix whatever this was, but the cost might be high. So high, we'd be forced to teleport the fuck out of here and start over elsewhere.

CHAPTER SIX, DAMIEN

I sat on a flat rock in a cave well north of Seattle. A troll, a dwarf, and a Druid ranged in a circle facing me. It had been years since I'd summoned them, and it pleased me they'd been willing to drop whatever they were doing to join me. If I'd learned anything during my years working for my people, it was bridge building. Hard to put a price on loyalty.

I'd always treated my spies with respect and rewarded them handsomely from the Fae coffers. Not that I still had instant access to that kind of wealth, but they didn't know my role had changed.

Nor would they.

Everyone's time was valuable, so I didn't pussyfoot around. "I'm looking for information about the local Coven. Has anyone heard anything?"

Eyebrows shot up. Except the troll. They're made of

stone and lack any sort of hair. "The witches?" he rumbled.

"Aye, the same," I said.

The Druid narrowed sky-blue eyes and gathered heavy black robes closer around his thin frame. Thick brown hair had been braided out of the way. "I wondered if anyone would ask after them," he murmured. "Curious events reached our attention."

"Curious, how?" I jumped in.

"Not sure. The harder the brotherhood looked, the more fell forces rebuffed us."

The fine hairs on the back of my neck prickled. "What kind of fell forces?"

"Not sure about that, either. It wasn't anything we could identify, but it kept us at bay as surely as if they'd threatened us directly."

"Do either of you know anything?" I asked the troll and the dwarf. When they shook their heads, I thanked them for meeting me and dismissed them.

The dwarf hung around, not subtle but persistent. I knew what he wanted.

"You'll get your silver," I told him. "Next time I see you."

He grumbled before shambling away muttering about perfidious Fae. He'd get over himself. And I'd make a point of visiting our coffers and fulfilling my promise. Of course, he hadn't contributed anything, so he wouldn't receive much.

I turned to Roland. "The witches are up to something, but their actions are shrouded?"

"Aye, about the size of it. It worried us, but not enough to dig deeper."

"Would you be willing to?" I sat back, gazing at him.

"What's in it for the brotherhood?"

"Depends. Name your price, and I'll run it past my council."

He probed me with magic. I held myself open. What I'd said had been true. If something was up with the Coven, I would indeed let my council know. And we always paid our informants.

"Two hundred gold pieces."

I winced. Before I could protest, he hurried on. "Something isn't right with all this. Repercussions could damage us."

I sucked in a breath and held out a hand. He clasped it and turned to leave. "Let me know what your council decides."

It went against the grain, but my next stop had to be Faery. Unlike my trip the previous evening, this time I scattered magic in an arc to alert my kinsmen I'd breached the veils. Rather than the library, which sits off by itself, I headed for rooms where we tend to socialize and share meals.

Logan pushed up from where he sat at a round table with half a dozen other Fae, all men but one. Fair hair cascaded down his back in curls. Sharp features were marked by almond-shaped silver eyes. He's always preferred robes. Tonight, his was snow-white sashed in gold and embroidered with runic markings in many colors.

"Back so soon?" He walked to where I stood and clasped a fist to his breastbone.

It was our traditional greeting; I mirrored his movements. My burly build is an anomaly amongst Fae. Most are like Logan: tall, slender, wispy almost, with sculpted features and slanted cheekbones.

"Aye, back so soon," I agreed.

He motioned to me to join the group at his table. I recognized all of them, but of course I would. After a round of greetings, someone must have ordered a tankard of mead because one floated through the air, clunking into place before me.

"Are you hungry?" Logan asked.

I shook my head.

"Have you decided to return?" Maeve trained ice-blue eyes on me. She's one of our resident seers. White hair hung to shoulder level where she'd gathered it into a thick queue. Black robes spread around her gaunt figure.

I smiled. "Surely, you of all people would know my intentions."

"If I were looking." She smiled back. "Which I haven't been."

"Are you going to tell us why you're here?" Logan

arched a fair brow. "Or will this be a game of twenty questions?"

Surprise rolled through me at the game analogy. "Been spending time on Earth?"

"Someone has to," he countered.

So they had replaced me. Kind of. Logan is more of a live-and-let-live sort. It would take something earth-shattering for him to feel the need to intervene.

"You were more effective," Maeve said flatly. It earned her a sour look from Logan. "Are you returning, or not?"

Scrambling to secure the best way to proceed, I bought a wee bit of time with questions. "Does everyone want me to?"

"What do you think?" Logan scowled. "None of the rest of us enjoy hobnobbing with mortals."

I did my damnedest to muffle a snort. It came out sounding like a dying goose. Before anyone commented, I muttered, "Why in the goddess's name would any of you think I liked spying for our people? I quit, didn't I?"

"Not for hundreds of years, you didn't," Logan said.

My next question was critical. "Have there been any incidents since I left?"

Logan curled his upper lip. "Could have been. I made short work of them."

"What does that mean?" I nailed him with my gaze, not willing to let him off the hook.

His pale cheeks sported red blotches. "I might have killed whomever. Easier that way. Cleaner too."

Outrage pounded a path from the crown of my head to the soles of my feet. I stood and faced him. "You killed without checking facts?"

He sprang upright, quivering with outrage. "I did what was necessary. You will not question me."

No matter how he blustered, guilt oozed from him. He'd picked the most expedient route, not the ethical one, and it gnawed at him.

"Are you coming back?" Maeve asked for a third time.

They wanted something from me. I wanted something from them. It's the stuff bargains are made of. I sank back into my chair; Logan did the same.

"I would consider returning, but not in the same way as I was here before," I began.

"What does that mean?" Logan narrowed his silver eyes. I felt probing where he attempted to cull my thoughts. Not going to happen. I slapped a ward into place.

"It means I have a life on Earth. I can do Fae-related work, but I won't give up my current life."

"How can you do both?" Maeve threaded her snowy brows into a thin line.

"Easily. I maintained an abode on Earth before. The only difference was I spent more time in Faery than I'm planning to do now."

"Why?" Logan continued to stare at me. "Surely, Faery offers superior creature comforts."

"I am not willing to upend the life I've spent years building. I owe you no explanations beyond that."

Maeve had extracted a crystal orb from the depths of her robes. Chanting softly, she rolled it between her hands.

Oh-oh. No hiding from her prescience.

I jumped in before she revealed my motives. "You may rescind your invitation before I'm done," I told the small group. Others who'd heard us talking had drawn near. We numbered closer to twenty than six.

"I met a witch in my lodging house. She and her familiar, a white wolf, were evicted from their Coven under mysterious circumstances—"

"Now, see here." Logan was back on his feet, shaking a finger my way. "We do not involve ourselves outside Fae blood. Whatever happened with this witch is none of our affair."

Murmurs of assent swelled through the rapidly growing group.

The old me—the one who'd walked away years ago—would have played the same hand. The new me was sick of folding when Fae rules tripped me up.

"I understand all that," I told him. "But I've never agreed with it. There's something suspicious about the Seattle Coven, and I aim to get to the bottom of it."

I didn't remember standing, but I was. Making a point to look everyone in the eye, I turned slowly, nodding at my kinsmen.

"I forbid it," Logan thundered.

"How?" I shot back. "You're only one. You do not speak for the council. And even if they say no dice too, I can still do what I want on my own time. If you want me to resume my duties—and it appears you need me in that role—I plan to utilize our resources to solve the witch problem."

Maeve looked up from her mini crystal ball. "It won't end well," she proclaimed.

I leveled my gaze her way. "Care to say more about that?"

A small shrug. "I can't. All I see is lots of blood."

"Can you tell whose?" Logan's question held a strangled quality. Squeamish of him since he'd all but admitted to killing willy-nilly.

The seer shook her head. Furrows formed in her high forehead. "Someone doesn't want me digging. It clouds the imagery."

Alarm bells tolled. "Same thing a Druid said," I told her.

"Huh? Why do you even know one?" she asked.

"During my years spying for our people, I cultivated a network of informants. He was one of them."

"Would have been nice to know," Logan groused.

"You never asked," I reminded him. "It isn't as if I purposely hid anything from you. And you've always known where to find me."

"What are we missing?" Maeve asked.

"Nothing."

"Why is this witch important enough for you to bend our covenant about non-interference?"

It was a fair question deserving of a well-thought-out answer. "I don't know her well, but something about her caught my attention. She has no one. The Coven kicked her out with the clothes on her back—and her familiar. They tried to separate them, but the wolf wasn't having it."

"Maybe she did something wrong," Logan posited. "Something you know nothing about and she's not telling you."

I shook my head. "Nice try. I swept her mind. The predominant impression was confusion." Blowing out a breath, I aimed for honesty when I added, "She has a flaw. Her eyes are mismatched. So are her wolf's. For a long while—her whole life—she employed a glamour to conceal the problem. When she tired of pouring magic into altering her appearance and dropped the veil, it took her sisters less than twenty-four hours to show her the door."

"Seems odd," Maeve murmured.

"More than odd," a few more Fae chimed in.

"Aye, to me as well," I told them. "She was convinced it was her eyes until she ran into a spectral sending from her mother, who was clear the problem ran far deeper."

"So the timing of her ouster was coincidence?" Logan asked.

"Apparently, except I don't believe in them," I told him.

"Me, either," he muttered.

At last, common ground and something we agreed on.

"I fear the Seattle Coven is mixed up with evil," I went on.

"Even if they are, how is it our problem?" Maeve tucked her crystal away.

"I will do everything in my power to keep the Fae out of this," I told her.

"Good luck." She scowled. "If you go poking around, it will have our magic stamped all over it."

"Which is why I've always employed a network of spies. The Druids will dig for me. For a price."

Logan spun one hand in a get-on-with-it gesture.

"Two hundred gold pieces."

He whistled long and low. "Did you spend that kind of coin before?"

"You mean when I was your primary spy?" At his nod, I went on, "Sometimes. The Druids have heard rumors all is not right with the witches. They're concerned about their safety. Ergo, the inflated price for more intel."

I was running out of time. Nights weren't long enough to lead a double life. One of these days, I'd need to catch a few hours' rest, but it wouldn't be this evening.

"I need to leave soon," I said. "Do what you must. Run this past the council. Scry to your heart's content. I shall return"—I'd started to say tomorrow night, but it might not be that soon—"when I can for your answer. Meantime, would you consider a loan of the gold pieces? So I can get that part of things underway?"

I still owed the dwarf and the troll for showing up. Not much. I'd take care of it myself.

"We can do that," Logan said gruffly. "I'll convene the council. You should have your answer within a matter of hours."

Maeve held up a hand. "Wait until I meet with Bess and Zoe. Our power is additive. Together, we should see more clearly than me on my own."

"What will you be looking for?" Logan asked her.

A corner of her mouth twisted downward. "Mostly whether Damien's actions will force us into a war with the Coven."

"Or whoever's behind them," I reminded her before I turned and strode from the room. "Good to see everyone despite the checkered circumstances," I called over one shoulder.

Daybreak had been hours ago when I returned to my lodging. At least I was in time for breakfast. When I strode into the full dining room, I didn't see Morgan or Zeke. Not immediate cause for alarm, so I filled my plate with the small amount of food left on the back table.

After I settled in to eat—and I was hungry—I searched for Morgan. Expending magic always spurs the appetite, but mine withered once it became clear she was nowhere in the building.

Had she taken advantage of my absence to leave?

She'd worried she was a problem, but I hadn't believed she'd vanish.

Fae are decent trackers, but like any magic, it works best before the trail grows too cold.

I stuffed the rest of an omelet sitting in congealed grease into my mouth, dropped my dishes in the plastic bins on the back table, and hustled from the room. Not for the first time, I blessed the relative anonymity of this particular boardinghouse.

Everyone had secrets, so no one was interested in mine.

I'd be late for work. If it happened too many times, they'd fire me, but construction jobs were plentiful. I'd find another position. Hell, if my people fell into line and accepted my gambit, I'd quit my outside employment. There wouldn't be time to do both.

On the front steps, I tossed power into a wide arc. Morgan's essence lit the world. I followed her path at a dead run. Was she in trouble? Had the witches decided evicting her wasn't enough?

Fury scoured me as I ran, curling my hands into fists. Defensive magic rose to my call, crackling between my hands. Fae council or no, I'd dish out enough misery to make those Coven bitches sorry they'd ever mounted a broomstick.

CHAPTER SEVEN, MORGAN

I stuffed my apron into a thick patch of shrubbery as I ran toward Zeke. I'd left in such a rush, I'd forgotten to remove it. Strategies collided, bouncing off the edges of my mind as I did my best to come up with a plan. Clearly, the wolf was visible. He'd moved beyond the reach of my glamour, so tossing it over him now would be counterproductive.

All it would do was label both him and me as magical creatures. Word would filter back to Smythe, who'd have an "I told you so," moment. Just before he instructed me to hit the bricks.

Sheesh. Being rejected was becoming a theme. Not one I wanted to reflect my life, but I couldn't seem to escape it.

After trying out and discarding multiple possibilities, the one I settled on was snatching Zeke into a teleport spell and getting the hell out of there. Meanwhile, I disguised myself. If no one recognized me, I might pull the fat out of the fire.

This time.

What had Zeke been thinking? Had he gone hunting and lost track of where he was? Not very fucking likely. The wolf was too smart to do something like that.

No point in conjecture. He'd tell me once we were back in the same place.

I was definitely closing on him. Only a few more blocks. I checked my appearance. Not bad. I was a shortish blue-eyed blonde with a scattering of freckles. My stinky clothing could belong to anyone. It would work in my favor since a crowd would shy away from me.

The stench of stale grease layered on top of body odor. I could have done something about it, but it wasn't in my best interest. By now, the cook had surely gone looking for me—and lodged a complaint with Smythe about me disappearing.

What could I tell him? It had to be believable, particularly if he'd searched the residence and not located me. When I latched onto a reason, it seemed plausible. I'd tell him I'd gotten my period. Lacking anything to deal with it, I'd run out in search of a market.

Female issues tend to make men like him uncomfortable. Hopefully, uncomfortable enough he'd drop the whole thing.

One problem more or less solved.

I slowed my pace. Zeke was close enough, I heard frantic yips.

By Hecate's breath, what had happened to him?

I readied a teleport spell, preparing to drape it over him and leave. I'd sort out the finer points later. One more block passed. I rounded the corner and stifled a scream.

Zeke was lashed to a post with wire. Blood welled where it cut into his skin and dripped onto the pavement. Two uniformed men held weapons trained on him.

"Stay put until animal control shows up," one barked at him.

"Yeah, be a shame to shoot you," the other snarled in a tone leaving zero doubt he'd love to pull the trigger and be done with it.

Moans drew my attention to three wounded women curled into bloody balls not far from Zeke. Holy godhead! They were witches. I bit my lower lip so hard I tasted blood to hold myself back from diverting the magic in my spell to pummel them senseless.

They'd hurt my wolf, my darling.

Pull it together, an inner voice growled.

The roar of an approaching siren was a call to action. I altered the weave of my spell to make damn good and sure it would defeat the wire around Zeke. Better to cut it first. So far, no one was paying me the slightest heed. I was just one more passerby gawking at the sideshow.

Perfect.

Edging closer, I caught his eye. He froze, wilting beneath my stare.

"Never mind about any of that," I told him. *"Do not fight my magic."*

A squarish black van type affair with Animal Control in the center of an emblem skidded around the corner. It was now or never. I pushed my spell over the wolf. It got the witches' attention. They stopped rocking and moaning long enough to search the area, hunting for the source of the spell.

"Good luck with that," I muttered and ignited my casting. I pushed hard, giving it everything I had. If I wasn't successful, the men piling out of the van carrying what looked like stun guns would cart Zeke off to goddess only knows where. I'm not particularly sensitive to iron, but he is.

My spell fought hard for ascendency; something pushed it back. I tried again. And again. We'd almost make it out of there, but something got in the way. The men with stun guns were closing on Zeke but not as quickly as before.

The obvious play of magic around him made them uncomfortable.

Hackles shot up the length of his back. He drew his upper lip back and snarled, showing full fang. Damned wolf always had a flair for the dramatic.

"Help me!" I shouted at him and poured air into my casting. Way more than I'd started with. When it didn't

do the trick, I beefed up the earth component. I was firing blind. Tossing everything at my disposal at the wall and hoping to fuck it did the trick.

All I needed to do was move us out of here.

"It's her." One of the witches pointed dead at me.

"Takes one to know one, Mirabelle," I sneered back.

Dancing on the balls of my feet, I selected a better vantage point. Maybe it was a lynchpin, or perhaps all the crap I'd fed into my fledgling spell finally hit terminal velocity. The city street shimmered and faded leaving Zeke and me floating in darkness.

Breath spurted from me. I uncurled my fingers from where they'd formed claws. The wolf, all 150 pounds of him, was in my arms. Remaining upright took stamina, determination. He panted but didn't cry out. Clearly, he'd been hurt.

"I'll kill those bitches," I muttered.

"Not if I get to them first," he wheezed.

Relief sluiced through me along with his mind voice. "Are you all right?" I demanded.

"Not really, but I will be."

My spell cried out for a destination. Could I chance my room? What if Smythe was there? With limited choices, I directed the journey magic to leave us in Damien's room. I'd confronted him there, but even if I hadn't it would have been simple to locate. No one else in the building had a scrap of magic, nothing obvious, anyway.

Breathe caught in my throat as the walls of his chamber shaped up around us. He wasn't here, but I hadn't expected him to be. After a cursory examination, where I patched Zeke as I found cuts, I said, "Remain here. I have to mend some bridges."

He got his feet under him, shook himself, and padded to a sink in the corner. I knew what he wanted and turned on the cold tap. He drank for a long while. As soon as he was done, I repeated myself.

"Stay here. I'll return for you as soon as I can."

"No worries on that front."

His words made me smile. Some life lessons cut deeper than others. I'd find out later how the witches had trapped him. To be on the safe side, I shored up the glamour, making certain it obliterated every trace of wolfiness.

While I was at it, I withdrew the glamour that had changed me into a blonde. The witches wouldn't have been fooled, but no one would listen to them if they prattled on about one of their own using magic to alter her appearance.

Besides, they wouldn't say a word. Maintaining a guise of being human meant not knowing about things like glamours and enchantment.

After checking through the door to make certain the hallway was empty, I let myself out and headed for the kitchen. My first stop had to be apologizing to the cook.

He was bent over a double sink full of dishes and

didn't notice me until I walked into his line of vision. "I can take over now," I said with a wan smile.

"Damn straight you can." He angled a pointed look my way and moved over.

I sank my arms into tepid, greasy water and picked up where he'd left off.

"What the hell happened to you?" he demanded.

I kept my gaze glued on the sink and manufactured a blush. "I, erm, had female problems. Nothing here, so I had to find a market."

"You could've said something," he muttered.

"Yeah, but I was embarrassed."

He swatted my butt and walked out of the kitchen.

Relief swirled in the pit of my stomach. One hurdle crossed. He wasn't mad at me. I'd run Smythe down later.

Turned out, he saved me the trouble. Well before I was done washing dishes, he strode into the kitchen. "Charles told me what happened. You should have said something. I've been looking for you for over an hour."

I started to ask why. Instead, I mumbled, "Sorry. Won't happen again."

"Where's the dog?"

His question surprised me, but it shouldn't have. If he'd been looking for me, surely, he'd have checked my room. I'd already established he felt he could enter my quarters as he choose.

This time, I didn't have to fake a blush. One bloomed

from my neck, sweeping to the top of my head until my skin felt like it was on fire.

"Uh, in Damien's room."

I stole a glance at Smythe. Shock reflected in raised eyebrows and an open mouth. "Two of you didn't waste much time," he muttered before turning to leave.

I came close to calling him back, to telling him he had it all wrong, that Damien and I were friends, nothing more.

I didn't. What passed between Damien and me or any tenants in this establishment wasn't Smythe's affair. I'd have to catch Damien up to speed tonight, but it was the least of my problems.

When I was done in the kitchen, I hustled back to his room and moved Zeke back to our quarters. Once we were settled, I draped a sloppy sound shield around us and said, "What happened?"

He'd made a decent recovery—if you didn't count multiple scabs crisscrossing his flesh beneath his thick fur. Claws clicked on the floor as he paced in small circles, tail pluming.

"I was a block away from here, standing in a grove of trees enjoying the day, when witch enchantment brushed me. I assumed it was you, so I opened myself to it."

A low growl reverberated in his throat. Hackles raised to half-mast. *"By the time I recognized Mirabelle, Zora, and Peony, they had me in their clutches. I fought as hard as I could, but they dragged me to the spot you found me and lashed me to that tree with iron.*

"The harder I struggled, the more it cut me. When blood flowed, soaking into the ground, the witches used it to bind me tighter."

"Hecate damn them to Hell for all eternity," I gritted. "Did they say why they captured you?"

Zeke's head bobbed. *"They wanted me back at the Coven. If I'd gone willingly, they'd have loosed me."* He paused, growling louder. *"When I refused, they stripped off the glamour. What followed was predictable."*

I knelt next to him and wrapped my arms around his neck. "You've left something out."

His eyes stared into mine, the soul of innocence. *"Like what?"*

"How'd Mirabelle and them end up hurt and on the ground."

Zeke's jaws spread in a lupine smile. *"They didn't believe me when I said no, so I followed my refusal with action. I should have done more damage. Lots more."*

"No shit."

He folded into a furry heap in front of me and licked my hands. *"They won't give up,"* he said.

No. They wouldn't. The question of the hour was why they wanted Zeke. He'd already told them he wouldn't tolerate being separated from me. Still, they'd pressed the matter. Maybe Mother was onto something when she'd said it wasn't our eyes.

"Did you square things with the man?" Another lick.

I nodded. "For now, he believed me."

"What should we do? We must be prepared."

Zeke was referring to the next salvo from the Coven. Apparently, booting me wasn't the end of things. I stroked his head, tangling my fingers in his rough outer coat.

"I don't know," I replied. "We'll come up with something. Meanwhile, you'll have to stay inside when I'm working."

He whined, not liking my edict but understanding why it was necessary.

My door flew open. Damien stomped inside, kicking the door shut in his wake. With brute force, he dragged the edges of my sound shield so it encompassed him too.

"There you are," he panted. "I tracked you. Found the place everyone's milling about like a bunch of idiots including three witches who were trying their damnedest to pass as mortals while fingering you and Zeke as black-magic wielders."

Laughter rolled from me. "I covered who I was. No one would see this me"—I tapped my chest—"and put two and two together."

"I blew holes in their tale telling," he said. "Removed their glamours until they looked witchy as hell. The mortals couldn't wait to shoo them away. Whole lot of smartphones took pictures. None of those women will be able to go anywhere unless they're glamoured-up to the nines."

"Thanks."

"Your blood was under a tree." Damien eyed the wolf. "Why'd they capture you?"

"Long story," I cut in. "More pertinently, Smythe cornered me since I'd skuttled out of kitchen duty to go after Zeke. When he asked where my dog was, I told the truth."

Damien's dark brows shot up. "And where was that?"

"Your room."

I cringed, waiting for him to chastise me for taking advantage of him. It never came. What he did was smile, say, "Quick thinking," and settle on the floor next to us.

"Smythe was quick to jump to, um, conclusions," I murmured.

"He would. Men are like that."

Damien ran his fingertips over the back of my hand. It sent electricity arcing through my body. "What you did was fine. No worries from me. You have bigger fish to fry."

"Don't I know it."

Zeke whined and licked Zeke's hand.

"Do you think they're done?" Damien angled his head to one side.

I shook my head. "Not even close."

"Why'd they want Zeke?"

"Don't know that, either," I admitted.

"We have some serious digging to do," he said.

I frowned. "I do, but why would it include you? You have a life, hopefully a less eventful one than mine."

"Because I have resources. I floated helping you past the Fae last night. They're considering it."

"If they say no, which is likely?"

He folded his big hand around mine. "Then we'll do this without them. I still have full access to the Fae library and my network of spies—"

"Your what?" I broke in, fighting incredulity. Why would Damien need a network of spies?

Was throwing my lot in with him a mistake? I didn't know him at all.

"Like what happened to Zeke, it's another long story," he replied. "With the goddess's grace, we'll have time to catch one another up—on everything."

Zeke placed his muzzle on top of Damien's hand and sighed. The wolf trusted him. Why was I having such a hard time?

I didn't want to box myself into a corner where he was my only ally. Not until I had a whole lot more information.

Out of the frying pan, into the fire ran through my mind. In one side, out the other.

Damien must have been listening in because he said, "I would never hurt you. I've gone out on a limb with my kinsmen to shine a light on why the Coven is acting so strangely."

I tugged my hand from beneath his and trapped his gaze with my own. "You'll have to give me time. All this is new for me. I've never lived outside a Coven guild house.

It's hard to sort who to trust, and I can't afford to make any mistakes."

"I understand. Can you lay your qualms aside long enough to strategize ways to keep you and Zeke safe while we're figuring out the rest?"

Despite efforts to hold a neutral expression, I smiled. "Yes. I can do that."

"Excellent. I'm two hours late for work, actually pushing three. How about if you stick close until late afternoon. Before the night's out, we'll have at least a few things in place to ensure whatever transpired today doesn't happen again."

Zeke yipped approval. I nodded slowly and got to my feet. Damien stood and wrapped his arms around me. His lips brushed my forehead, and then he was gone.

The feel of his nearness seared me. Images of his mouth teasing mine, of his hands roaming my body lit a fire in my nether regions. Witches aren't strangers to sex. We pleasure ourselves plenty. It's only men we steer clear of. Before I could settle in and spin an erotic fantasy of Damien and all the things we'd do for one another, my door flew open once more.

Smythe stood beneath the lintel, taking in Zeke and me. "Be in the kitchen at four," he instructed. "So you can help with dinner. Where's that mending?"

Bending, I handed him the finished stack, gathering the items I'd been using for bedding. "Any chance I could get a mattress?" I asked.

He scanned the small room as if surprised such a basic item would be missing. "Sure. I'll have maintenance drop something off before tonight."

The door clicked shut. I sank to a crouch, rubbing my eyes. I had lots of questions and painfully few answers. A nap was in order, and then I'd escort Zeke outdoors so he could hunt.

"I'll hold you to it," the wolf said.

I ruffled his fur. "I'm sure you will."

CHAPTER EIGHT, DAMIEN

Luck was running my way. The foreman wasn't anywhere to be found when I slid into work as unobtrusively as possible. Because I swathed myself in don't-look-here spells, no one commented on my tardy arrival.

The day passed quickly since my mind was occupied with how to proceed. My first guess was the witches I'd exposed had captured Zeke. Somehow Morgan found out and had ridden to the rescue.

Of course, she'd found out. They were linked.

I had to get to the bottom of the Coven's odd behavior. In all my reading, I'd never come across even a single instance where they'd jettisoned a fully fledged witch from their ranks.

Another problem was my feelings for Morgan. What had begun as a Sir Galahad move was rapidly shifting to something more complex. I cared about her, was attracted to her in a way that ran far deeper than wanting to rescue her from her kinswomen.

She had feelings for me, but she was fighting them. The rumors floating around about witches remaining celibate and unattached must be true. They did create new witches, but not very many. Today, they had ways to procure sperm and didn't have to deal with men at all. Who knows what they did a hundred years ago.

The unfortunate men probably never lived long enough to tell anyone about their forced time amidst witches.

A board clattered out of my hands, narrowly missing two men on scaffolding. "Fuck. I am so sorry." Loosening the rope that held me in place, I dropped low enough to recapture the errant board.

"Dude. Are you trying to kill us?" one grunted.

His harness wasn't clipped to the safety rope. I pointed at it.

"Nag. Nag. Nag," he mumbled, but did run a carabiner through the loop on the front of his harness.

I'd started back to my perch with the board, intent on nailing it into place when the other worker yelled, "Hey. Where were you earlier?"

"Right here." I inserted a jaunty note into my reply and made certain he'd believe me with a splash of magic.

"Eh, my memory's going."

The fellow next to him slugged his upper arm. "Lay off the hooch, dude."

"Mind your own business. You're not my mother."

I left them to it and positioned enough boards to move to the next segment of this project. Once the exterior was done, we'd transition inside and slap drywall into place. When it was done, this would be a smallish apartment building and far from a fancy one.

It was nearing five. I sorted tools, organizing them so they'd be ready for me tomorrow. We all had our own toolboxes. I kept mine locked, not so much worried about someone stealing from me but loathe to have anyone else's grimy paws on my things. I'd wrapped the most important tools in spells. If another touched them, they'd sustain a nasty shock.

"Damien," floated up to me.

I glanced at the foreman. He balanced on the same scaffolding as the two workmen I'd nearly clonked with the board. His orange hard hat reflected the rays of the setting sun.

Waving to acknowledge him, I finished putting my tools in the box and locked it. He was about to make a pitch for overtime. Sometimes, I took the bait. Tonight wasn't going to be one of them.

"Feel like a spot of overtime?" he continued.

"Sorry, Jerry. Not tonight."

"Aw, come on, Damien. This project is behind schedule."

Because you hire the cheapest of the cheap.

"Sorry," I repeated. "I can't help you tonight. I have plans, and I can't change them."

"Tomorrow night, then?"

"Perhaps. We'll see what tomorrow brings. Back at it bright and early." Before he could whine and wheedle, I released the breaker bar and rappelled to the ground. Once there, I unclipped from the rope and stripped off my harness, dropping it into one of many common bins where we kept our gear.

My next stop was Faery, but I couldn't teleport from here. After turning down several offers to lift a few at a nearby tavern, I loped along the warren of streets zigzagging this way and that uphill from West Seattle's beaches. As soon as I located a likely alley, I ducked into it crafting a spell on the fly.

When it cleared, I stood outside the library where I'd researched witches. The hallway was deserted, so I hustled to the common area where I'd been the previous evening.

Logan and three other council members sat at a round table. Maeve was with them. Excellent. Without waiting for an invitation, I joined them.

"What did your scrying reveal?" I asked without preamble. "Did adding Bess and Zoe sharpen your foreseeing?"

Maeve arched a white brow. "What? No nice to see you or how've you been?"

"I just saw you last night. If there's something I need to know, please tell me."

"He said please," Logan pointed out.

"So he did," Maeve murmured.

Sheesh. Was I usually so insufferably rude, my use of please rose to the surface as cause for commentary?

"Simpler to show you," she said and swiped a hand downward.

A shimmery screen hovered in the air. Runes danced around it. I dragged a chair across from the display, sat in it, and watched carefully.

An old rambling mansion formed. Wings angled out in many directions, some topped with turrets. Had to be the Coven guild house since it oozed with witchy enchantment. Gardens filled with exotic plants surrounded the place. Greenhouses lined the southern exposure. A tall black fence with pointy posts limited both access and a view from the street.

The scene shifted to inside, leaving the old brick façade behind. Twelve witches were arrayed at a shiny black oblong table in an opulent room. Thick rugs lined wooden floors. A fire crackled in a huge fireplace with a green marble hearth. Metal sculptures of witches casting spells, witches flying, witches tending to animals stood in every corner and alcove. Paintings graced the walls.

Between the paintings and sculptures, the history of witches played out.

A chandelier made up of hundreds of lit candles was suspended from a coved ceiling.

One of the witches from earlier today rose to her feet and shook a fist at her sisters. Dark hair had been cropped to shoulder level. Earlier, she'd been clad in street clothes, but now a white robe swathed her bony body. "None of you followed my directions. Because of your insolence, we failed today."

"I resent that." Another witch, this one with flame-red curls, surged to her feet and squared off in front of the dark-haired one.

"Resent away." Witch One waved a dismissive hand. "You weren't there."

Another witch chopped a hand through the air. "We do no one favors by bickering amongst ourselves." She shoved heavy black hair behind her shoulders. "I told you at the front end of this it was a mistake to target the wolf. He'll never relinquish his bond with Morgan."

"How else will we retrieve him?" Witch One asked.

"We don't have to," Witch Three insisted.

I watched the scene unfold. Was it happening in real time? Or had Maeve captured it earlier and was replaying it for my edification?

"Um, we certainly do," Witch One insisted. "As long as he's with Morgan, she's impregnable."

"Then we should have just tossed her in the dungeons," another witch, this one fair, jumped into the discussion.

"Easier said than done. You may recall the only dungeons strong enough to hold one of us are in the Old Country." Witch One glared at her kinswomen.

"I want to hear the prophecy again," the redhaired witch announced. "They're cloaked in riddles. Perhaps we missed something."

"We did not," Witch One proclaimed.

"I want to hear it again, anyway," Witch Two pressed. Running her gaze around the room, she snapped her fingers. "Who's with me?"

Hands shot up.

Witch One shook her head. "Fine. Someone run and fetch Lilith."

While we waited for scene two to unfold, I murmured, "Not so different from our process."

Logan grunted. "You stole the thoughts from my mind. If their actions weren't so egregious, I'd almost feel sorry for the one leading their council."

Someone must have lit a fire under Lilith. A frail witch who looked like she wasn't a day over fourteen entered the room at a dead run. Sinking to her knees the moment she cleared the entrance, she bowed her head. Black hair streaked with golden highlights fanned around her, creating a shroud. Unlike her sisters, she wore modern garb: jeans and an oversized cream-colored fisherman's knit sweater. Her feet were bare and filthy.

"Get up," Witch One thundered.

Lilith shot upright but avoided eye contact. A shock

riffled through me. Her eyes were the same color as Morgan's white one. Was it a genetic aberration? Was she blind?

"Where's your sphere?" Witch Two demanded.

"Right here." Lilith raised both hands. A glowing crystal ball perhaps half a meter across appeared between them.

"Tell us again what you saw," Witch One ordered.

A glazed look passed over her odd eyes as she stared at the orb. Colors danced within its depths. Where her fingers pressed against it, they turned translucent, displaying blood pumping through arteries and veins.

Lilith didn't request clarification, which meant this vision was more important than any she'd conjured recently. She balanced from foot to foot; her eyes turned a brilliant blue.

When she spoke, it was a recitation without inflection.

"Since well before we left the Old Country, we have known a queen would rise. A witch who would rule witches in every Coven. All witches recognize this. Some welcome the idea. Others are opposed. Astrological forces aligned for Morgan's birth, but we ignored them because the rest of her didn't match the prophecy.

"Until she revealed her true self. Then we knew it had to be her—"

"We did not know," Witch Two cut in. "Might have

been coincidence. That mother of hers could have spelled her eyes to deceive us."

"For what reason?" Another witch, who'd been silent, sounded weary of the topic.

Witch One shrugged. "Power. If her spawn became queen, her role in our hierarchy would have expanded. Perhaps her hawk put her up to it."

"Farfetched, Mirabelle. Farfetched," Witch Two muttered. "If it were true, we'd have dredged it out of her. As things stand, we tortured one of our own for naught."

Mirabelle slapped a hand on the table. "I've had enough of your insolence."

Lilith still held the orb, but its inner light had faded. Perhaps it was sensitive to disagreements.

"Am I dismissed?" she asked in a low, breathy voice. Her eyes had shaded to white.

"No. Finish the prophecy," Mirabelle ordered.

Lilith nodded. "When Morgan attempted to draw the covens together under her leadership, warfare ensued. Long, bloody, unresolved. I never saw to the end of it. Her familiar had better luck. The animals listened to him, leaving their bondmates and joining an army with Zeke at its head. They fought for Morgan, but it only made things worse."

"Surely there's more," Mirabelle said after Lilith fell silent.

"No, mum. 'Tis all I've been afforded the privilege of viewing. More may come, but it has yet to arrive."

A finely woven net shimmered out of nowhere and clanked over Lilith's head. It had to be a truth spell.

The seer changed from a demure looking child prophet to a raving, shrieking bitch. Her hair sprouted snakes. Fangs grew. Long, curved ruby nails graced her hands.

"I am your prophet," she shrilled. "If you do not believe my words, why force aught from me? Withdraw your insulting truth spell. Immediately."

Tension tugged at every muscle. What manner of being was Lilith? Witches have never been shapeshifters.

Maeve chuckled. "Wish I could do that. Might keep the lot of you in line."

"Very funny." Logan skewered her with his silvery eyes.

"Fine. Have it your way." Mirabelle's voice drew my attention back to the wavery display.

The truth net vanished as quickly as it had arrived, leaving trails of whitish smoke in its wake.

"Better." Lilith placed her hands on her hips. The globe remained suspended in front of her. "Shall we go back to where I said, 'More may come, but it has yet to arrive.'"

The other witches fell into line without missing a beat. Did Lilith make a habit of mini rebellions?

The weary-sounding witch splayed her hands on the table and stood. Straight white hair cascaded to knee level. Black robes embroidered with plants and animals swathed her short, plump form. "If you speak true, it means we have no idea how this would have shaken out if we hadn't intervened.

"I am eldest amongst you," she went on. "I advised against the current course of action. And I most certainly advised against your ill-fated attempt to capture Zeke."

"But her enchantment is bound up with his," Mirabelle argued. "The only way to ensure she never comes into the full spectrum of her power is to separate them."

"Why do we want to tamper with destiny?" another witch asked.

"Aye," Witch Two jumped in. "Ever since we kicked Morgan out, I've seen naught but evil portents. My cat is in full agreement."

A mournful yowl from somewhere suggested said cat wasn't far away.

"Before I asked. In the face of your inexcusable lack of respect, I am leaving now with or without your permission." Lilith made a grab for her crystal orb and stomped from the room.

"Seen enough?" Maeve's words broke into my concentration.

I nodded; the screen winked out.

Maeve was breathing hard. The show and tell had blown through a considerable amount of enchantment.

"Thank you," I told her. "I appreciate how much power you expended on my behalf."

"You're welcome." She huffed out a breath. "You cannot tell her."

"Why not?"

"Because everyone and their dog has been tampering in Morgan's life and future," Logan answered for Maeve. "Forces are at play, and the Fae will not meddle with them."

"What would happen if you told her?" Maeve arched both brows my way. "She won't be able to do anything with the information, and she'll feel like she should. It will make her even more miserable than she already is.

"Her own Coven, the one place witches should believe in her, made her an outcast. How do you think other Covens will react?"

"Exactly," Logan tossed out.

"Besides," Maeve added. "Lilith left something major out. I'm not certain what, but she knows far more than she revealed. It has to be why she turned into a ravening monster when the others questioned her."

I blew out a tense breath. "So you're telling me to do nothing?"

"Be her friend." Maeve's voice was soft. "Support her and her wolf. If the Coven pulls any more shenanigans, mitigate the harm. Much like Lilith, I have yet to scry how this turns out."

"So she was telling the truth about that part?" Logan asked.

Maeve nodded and turned to face him. "I believe so.

You will not like this, but Damien crossed Morgan's path for a reason. Time will provide clarity. Meanwhile, she needs him."

"Something's not quite adding up," I muttered.

Maeve spun one hand in a get-on-with-it gesture; I organized my thoughts.

"Witches are guardians of the natural world. They wouldn't fight a prophecy—unless they'd joined forces with others."

"Like whom?" Logan asked.

I frowned. "Not sure. They tortured Morgan's mother, one of their own. Yesterday, they bound Zeke with wire that cut his flesh. Do either of those actions sound witchlike to you?"

A sea of head shakes met my question.

"Why wouldn't Lilith have mentioned dark allies?" Maeve asked.

"She might be bound to silence. The others would have kept such an association secret. Besides, if there is an alliance with evil, it would be a side affair. Surely, not every witch is part of it."

"I scry truth, secret or no," Maeve pointed out.

"Aye, you do. Lilith seemed not much more than a child."

Maeve jabbed me in the ribs. "She's well into her second century. Looks are deceiving."

I turned to our seer. "When you're asked to share a vision, can you leave things out?"

"Of course."

"So, Lilith may well know more than she's letting on."

"I already said as much. Or Mirabelle or one of the others has threatened her with mayhem if she spills that pot of beans," Maeve said darkly.

"Did you come to a decision about returning to work for us?" Logan changed the subject.

My life was in flux. There are no coincidences. Morgan had crossed my path for reasons I had yet to tease out. I'd be best positioned to help her with the Fae standing behind me.

"Aye, I will return to my previous duties. For a while, I will also continue my work among mortals."

"Why?" Logan asked.

"I'm not sure, but I'm going with my gut on this one."

"Tread carefully," Maeve cautioned.

"What have you seen?"

"Nothing yet. When I do—or Bess or Zoe—you'll be the first to know." She was on her feet with a small blade in hand.

I faced her. "What are you binding me to?"

"Silence. When I said you must not reveal aught of tonight to Morgan, I was serious."

"There's no need for a blood bond—" I began.

"I believe there is. Extend your arm."

When I walked out of Faery, magic was patching up the wound in my forearm. My mind was full. Rather than return to my lodging, I crossed the veils to Earth and walked for a while. Long enough to bury my newfound knowledge deep.

Keeping secrets from Morgan would come back to bite me. When she found out—and find out she would—she'd be hurt and angry. It couldn't be helped.

I had one job, and one job only: keeping her safe.

We had to find her mother and extricate her before the Coven did more damage. Morgan was already worried about her, so I could offer assistance without revealing anything more.

It had to be our next move, but I'd wait for her to float the idea. She'd already mentioned a visitation. I'd remind her of it and let events unfold. I tested the walls around my newly acquired knowledge, shored them up in a few spots, and set a path for the rundown lodging I called home.

Morgan was there. Longing for her filled me, and I quickened my pace.

CHAPTER NINE,
MORGAN

Zeke's romp had been uneventful, but then we hadn't strayed more than a couple of blocks from the building. He was in our room, curled on a mattress that had materialized during our absence. For the last half hour, I'd been working side by side with the cook.

Residents would begin filtering in for dinner soon. I kept expecting to see Damien, but he never dropped in for the evening meal. Hours passed, and I was finishing up washing dishes. The cook had been solicitous. It took a while for me to connect the dots. He associated the flow of moon blood with ill health.

I'd lied about that earlier, but were all mortal men so stupid? Had Smythe told him about Zeke being in Damien's room? Being the topic of gossip made me cringe.

On top of everything, unhappiness combed a bitter trail through me. I'd been looking forward to sitting with Damien and sharing a meal. As things stood, I'd grabbed a plate and eaten perched on a stool in the kitchen.

I kicked myself. Damien owed me nothing. He'd been kind to Zeke and me because he was a genuinely nice mage. Maybe he already had someone in his life and had gone to dinner with them. Or he'd been called back to Faery. No matter how I chided myself, I couldn't stop thinking about him.

The cook had left a while back. I folded my dish towel and walked through the darkened dining room. It was past time for Zeke to go outside. I wasn't as comfortable walking him at night, so we'd stick close to well-lighted areas. Magic flows strongest during the dark hours, and it wasn't like the sisterhood of witches to give up when their first attempt to do something was thwarted.

I still couldn't chop Damien out of my thoughts. It annoyed and confused me by turns. He'd disappointed me, but it wasn't a reason to not get on with my evening.

No one's fault but your own, an inner voice reminded me.

It was true. I'd made assumptions I shouldn't have. Those assumptions shredded my feelings. Granted I was still raw from losing my position in the Coven, but it was a weak excuse at best. Had I been more cautious, I'd have accepted tonight's events with more equanimity.

Hell, I wouldn't have batted an eyelash when Damien

didn't come to dinner. It wasn't as if we'd made plans. He owed me nothing. I was acting like a lovestruck teenager, not a centuries-old witch.

I squared my shoulders as I covered the distance to my room determined to do better next time. I could have opened the door with magic; instead, I fished a key out of my pocket and unlocked it. Best to get out of the habit of using magic for everything. What if someone saw me? I didn't want to spend my time making excuses and wiping memories.

When I pushed it open, Damien sat on the mattress with Zeke.

The wolf's head was in Damien's lap, and he was scratching his belly. Zeke's tongue lolled. He wore his happy face.

I pushed the door shut, feeling flustered. I'd longed for Damien, and here he was.

He stood and walked toward me. His ice-blonde hair was unbound and fell halfway down his back. He'd dispensed with the glamour that made his ears look human. They rose to graceful points. I wanted to stroke them in the worst way.

The rest of him too.

"Sorry I missed dinner." He smiled; it softened the austere planes of his face. His energy filled the room, bouncing off the walls, stealing my breath.

In the face of his sincerity and the sheer force of his presence, my vow to keep my distance disintegrated.

"Me too. I looked for you."

"I had business in Faery." He winced. "Oops."

A sound shield clattered around us, sealing out the world.

"No need for that," I said. "Time for Zeke's evening walk. We can talk outside."

Outside was a grand idea. If we remained here, I'd throw myself into his arms, run my fingertips along his ears, and discover how his lips would taste. Not the wisest move. I'd already misread him once.

The wolf jumped from his spot on the mattress, tail pluming. He'd had the run of the grounds at the Coven guild house and was probably missing his freedom.

Damien held out an arm, the invitation crystal clear. I'm ashamed I didn't hesitate so much as ten seconds before I hooked my hand into the crook of his arm. No one was in the hall or on the stairs.

We walked out the front door into a clear, cold night. I directed a flow of magic to keep myself warm. Clothes were still a problem, but I could have grabbed my coat. Would have were I not so entranced by the mage striding next to me.

I crafted a leash illusion. Zeke trotted by my side, stopping here and there to sniff and do doggie things.

"How about the park?" Damien asked.

"Sure."

The streets were crowded with the afterwork crowd stopping to shop or eating dinner in small cafes. We slipped into a small park; Damien altered the weave of reality. Suddenly, we were in the park but also in another space perhaps one world over. Witches aren't much for traveling off-world. I've done it, but not frequently.

"This should work," Damien said. "No one can hear us."

"Probably no one can see us, either," I commented.

"Aye. Better to err on the side of caution."

I released the magic holding my leash illusion together. Damien laced his fingers with mine. I shouldn't have let him, but the warmth of his hand was enticing. I wanted to touch him. And have him touch me. The sensation was new, heady. The Coven had kicked me out, so I wasn't bound by their rules any longer.

Rules like celibacy.

"I'll be returning to my work for the Fae," Damien explained. "But I'm not quite ready to quit my job here."

"What'd you do for the Fae? You alluded to it, but never provided details." If he didn't want me to know, he wouldn't answer.

"Two things. I kept a supply chain going, so we always had sufficient food and supplies."

"And the other?" We'd stopped walking and stood, facing one another.

"I worked undercover. Demons and vampires have always been a problem. I kept my ear to the ground. Whenever the possibility of trouble reared its head, I made certain the Fae council could mount a realistic response."

I angled my head to one side. It explained why he'd mentioned a network of spies. "Those sound important. Why'd you quit?"

"Several reasons, but mostly a lack of cooperation from my kinsmen. No one was willing to patrol with me—or do anything else. One day, I'd had enough. Walked out of Faery, and never returned—until recently. The Fae had to assign someone else to oversee the supply chain. They didn't bother to replace my other duties. Not entirely, that is."

"I bet they missed you."

No one should have eyes that green. Even in the dusky gloom of the park, they shone like finely cut gemstones. Thick, blond lashes framed them, long enough to brush his angled cheekbones.

"They say they did." He chuckled, draped an arm around my shoulders, and we started walking again.

"What changed? Why are you going back?"

I sucked in a breath. His answer was important, important enough I flirted with a truth net, but it would have been way out of line.

He squeezed my hand tighter. "You're why I returned to Faery a couple of nights back. I needed the Fae library. You're also why I resurrected my network of informants."

Heat rose to my cheeks despite the chilly night. I ground to a halt and pulled my hand out of his. "While I appreciate the gesture, you scarcely know me. I can work this out on my own."

He dropped his hands onto my shoulders. Warmth flowed downward, igniting needs I had no name for.

"Not how this works, and you know it." His voice was low, urgent. "There are no coincidences. Our paths crossed for a reason. Maeve, our seer, is in full agreement, and—"

"You told the Fae about me?" I spluttered, truly uncomfortable to have my personal business scattered through mageland.

"Aye, but for the best of reasons. I need their combined strength to help you."

I crossed my arms beneath my breasts to still the trembling in my stomach. "I never asked for your help."

He laughed. It was the last thing I expected. "You didn't, but you're getting it anyway. I'm tough to get rid of."

Zeke bounded out of the darkness, rose onto his haunches, and licked Damien's face. *"This will be good for us,"* he informed me before waltzing back to whatever he'd been up to.

"He trusts me," Damien said. "Why are you having such a hard time?"

Why was I?

"I'm, uh, used to working alone."

He snorted. "Right. What about the infamous sisterhood?"

Busted. "You're not going to let this go until I capitulate, are you?"

"Nope. I can be ingratiating, charming, even. And stubborn as fuck. You need a friend. Means you're going to have to trust someone. May as well be me."

"This is all so new, I'm not certain what I need."

"One more reason to team up with me. Come on, Morgan. You can always kick me to the curb later."

I took off at a lope. He fell in beside me. We ran laps around the park with Zeke yipping happily. Maybe it was doing something active together, but my reservations faded.

How bad could this be?

Horrible, an inner voice inserted. *What if he's not what he seems?*

Zeke would know, I answered myself.

If Damien was following my ramblings, he had the good sense to keep his snooping to himself. Speaking of internal dialogue, I could torture myself with this, or I could go with the flow. Trust the goddess would watch out for one of her own. Maybe Damien was right about our meeting being far more than coincidence.

"Okay," I said.

"Okay, what?" He stopped and spun me to face him.

"I accept your...your presence in my life."

Relief streamed from him in palpable waves. He hadn't been at all certain I'd acquiesce, no matter how confident he'd seemed. It told me something about him I hadn't known.

He wasn't arrogant, a huge plus in my book.

"You'd said you need ID?" He arched a fair brow.

I nodded. "Smythe is keeping me busy, but my payment is room and board. I need money. For that, standard ID documents would come in handy."

"Will you accept a loan from me?"

Would I? Not much choice.

"So long as we're both clear it's a loan."

"Fair enough. You can't get a decent paying job without ID. Ready to go back?"

I whistled. Zeke came at a dead run, zipped past, and circled us.

"More than ready. I should have brought my coat. Been using magic so I don't freeze."

Damien slipped a leather vest off his shoulders and dropped it in place over mine. "It will cut the chill."

"Thanks."

"It all flows together," he said.

"What flows together?"

"Once you have ID, we can find you a job. When you have money coming in, you can buy clothes. Fitting into the mortal world isn't all that hard, but you can't do it without resources."

I elbowed him. "Figured out that much on my own."

Power rippled across me as we crossed to the Earth

side of the park. It was deserted; rain sluiced from a cloud-covered sky.

"No point putting up with this," Damien murmured.

Fae enchantment swirled around me smelling of wildflowers and wet evergreen trees. When it cleared, we stood in my room, water pooling around us. Zeke shook droplets out of his coat, but he did it near the door. I draped his customary glamour over him.

Not that I was expecting Smythe, but I didn't want to be caught unprepared, either.

I felt the full weight of Damien's attention, intense and full of protectiveness. No one had guarded me since I was old enough to craft my own glamour to cover my mismatched eyes.

"Do you know who your father was?"

I took a step back, surprised by the question. "Of course not. Such information is secret."

"Surely, the Coven maintains birth records," Damien pressed.

"Yeah, but a single witch is in charge, and the logbooks are concealed with magic." I chewed my lower lip. "Why are you asking?"

Furrows formed between his brows. "I'm assuming your mother didn't have your eyes, which means they had to come from your father. If that's so, he was some type of mage."

"Never thought about it," I mumbled, feeling like an

idiot. "Why didn't I dig deeper? It would have been normal, expected even."

He touched my shoulder. "Keep looking for an answer. It's important. So's why Zeke's eyes are a match with yours."

Another mystery I hadn't probed. At all. I'd accepted Mother's rationale about bond animals matching their mistress's traits. Except none of the other bond animals did.

Bending, he brushed his lips across my forehead and was gone. It took a moment before it registered he hadn't bothered with the door.

I still had his vest. It smelled like him and was far softer than it looked. I started to take it off but couldn't bring myself to. Instead, I gathered the towel I'd been using for a washcloth and headed for the bathroom. It was empty as usual, so I snuck in a quick shower.

It was the first time I'd bathed since leaving the Coven. The feel of hot water pummeling me was soothing. Some kind soul had left a sliver of soap and a small bottle of shampoo. I was careful not to take too much. My towel was scarcely more than washcloth sized. I had to wring it out a few times before I was dry enough to put my smelly clothes back on.

Tomorrow, I'd find a way to wash them even if I had to use one of the sinks in the kitchen. The one in Damien's room wasn't big enough. Maybe he had a spare pair of pants and a shirt I could borrow for long enough to clean my garments. As a compromise, I rinsed out my stockings and underwear, draped them over an arm, and returned to my room.

Zeke had curled up next to the mattress. Considerate of him since his fur was still damp. I hung the wet items on hooks and undressed. No handy stack of mending to pile over me, but whoever left the mattress had also left a blanket and scratchy sheets that smelled of bleach. And a single lumpy pillow.

I did a crappy job making the bed. The day had caught up with me, and I was tired. After dousing the lamp, I crawled into bed.

And slithered right back out to retrieve Damien's vest. I folded it on top of the pillow and laid down. His scent excited and soothed me by turns. When I wasn't thinking about him, my thoughts turned to Mother.

She held secrets.

I understood why she hadn't disclosed any of them when I was a child, but she'd had hundreds of years to correct that and hadn't.

Why?

Where was she? Had the other witches extricated her from their ranks?

"She might need our help," Zeke said softly.

"We have to find her before we can do much good."

The more I tossed it back and forth, the more concerned I became. "We'll go back to the hills where she was waiting for us," I told the wolf.

All of her hadn't been there, but she'd opened a channel. If I could locate it, I should be able to communicate with her.

"Tomorrow, after breakfast," the wolf agreed.

Between having a plan and Damien's vest beneath my head, something tightly coiled within relaxed enough for sleep to claim me.

CHAPTER TEN, DAMIEN

I'd left Morgan's room in a hell of a hurry. If I hadn't, the temptation to crush her against me would have been too potent to walk away from. Tonight had unfolded better than I'd expected. I'd kept a close eye on her thoughts, so every nuance of her internal struggle had played out in living color.

When she'd come around to deciding maybe I wasn't the antichrist, relief filled every crevice of my being. I'd made a point to be obvious about it, so she'd never think I took any part of her for granted.

I was outside the building since I had a few things to do before morning. My first stop was the Druid guild house. I tapped on a stout wooden door. And tapped again. Fifteen minutes later, a disheveled brother appeared, tugging a brown robe around himself.

It wasn't all that late, but the brotherhood apparently retired early.

"Is Roland about?" I inquired.

The Druid who'd drawn door duty narrowed dark eyes. "Who's asking?"

"Damien."

The Druid sniffed audibly. "Fae, eh?"

I didn't dignify his question with a reply.

"What do you want with Roland?"

Great. Fine. We were off and running playing twenty questions.

"We have unfinished business. Please tell him Damien is here with favorable news."

The sound of bare feet slapping stones was followed by, "Move over, Micah." Roland pushed the other Druid aside. "Welcome. Apologies for my brother's rudeness."

Micah made a grunting sound and waddled away.

I tossed a quickie sound shield around us to discourage Micah or any other curious Druids from listening in. "The Fae agreed to your price," I told him.

"Excellent. I'll begin apace."

"My other piece of news," I went on, "is I will be resuming my duties for the Fae, so this will be the first of many assignments."

Brown brows shot up. "Wasn't aware you'd taken a hiatus."

"You are now. It's the reason work slowed so much."

"Why'd you choose to return?"

It was a fair question. "The witch conundrum drew me in. And 'tis high time I was true to my blood."

Roland nodded. "Understood. How will I contact you with information?"

"Same way you used to. I might not respond quite as quickly, but you will hear from me."

"I'm treading lightly," Roland reminded me. "Something isn't right here. If I plop into the middle of it, I might not escape."

"Take whatever precautions you deem necessary." I clapped a hand over my chest. He did the same.

A short hop returned me to my lodgings. Exercising restraint, I landed in my own room. Morgan and I would catch a few minutes over breakfast and map out the day. If I could finesse it, I'd set up a meeting between her and the document forger for tomorrow night. Results were instantaneous. Meant she'd have a driver's license, high school diploma, and a birth certificate before we left the waterfront dive he worked out of.

She'd also have at least some history attached to the documents. What he usually did was research recently dead who were the right gender and age, and who'd been so invisible in life no one who'd ever known them was likely to gum up the works.

His strategy had worked well for me. No one had ever questioned my phony credentials. Probably why he was so expensive. He guaranteed results, or he'd make another set for free.

I stared at my bed. I wasn't the least bit sleepy, but I should at least lie down. The last two nights had been a bust where rest was concerned. It convinced me my other agenda items, including a trip to Faery and a reconnaissance mission to the Coven guild house, could wait.

I'm an accomplished spy. Should be since I did it long enough. Morgan had mentioned birth records. Depending on how well warded the Coven was, I might be able to sneak inside, locate the records room, and explore Morgan's birth at my leisure.

I'd meant to ask her how old she was. It would shave time off my search. But women are particular about things like age, and I hadn't found a way to sneak it in. Perhaps it was enough I had her thinking about why she knew so little about her origins.

Someone had shielded them from her, probably her mother. If the little scene playing out at the Coven guild house was to be believed—and it had seemed real enough—Morgan's mother had pulled the wool over everyone's eyes.

Had she chosen to mate outside Coven strictures?

It would explain a lot.

I sat in a chair and pried off my boots. After hanging my damp garments on hooks, I dropped a nightshirt over my head and got into bed. Broken springs poked me; I positioned myself between them. This down-at-the-heels lodging had drawbacks, but the anonymity it afforded made up for a lack of creature comforts.

One of my magics is linked with the dreamworld. I trod paths leading to the Coven's guild house and explored how it was guarded.

Turned out not at all.

Witches must be an arrogant bunch to leave their dwelling open to any who turned the latch.

Too simple, an inner voice warned.

Aye, it was right. Loose security had to be a trap set to snare the unwary. What the hell did the women do with poor sods who stumbled into their territory? My imagination had a heyday with it until conjecture grew downright creepy.

It was something I could ask Morgan about. Whether she'd answer remained to be seen. She might be clinging to some misplaced loyalty despite their horrific treatment.

I rolled over and punched the pillow. After the little scene I'd watched earlier today, my respect for witches was in serious decline. Their seer turned into a latter-day Medusa if anyone crossed her.

What other secrets did the guild house harbor?

I'd find them all before I was done. What I did with them remained to be seen. It depended what kind of shape Morgan's mother was in when we located her.

Big talk.

Even if I discovered a conduit ran from the guild house straight to Hell, there wasn't any type of central registry with a set of standards all mages adhered to. Nope. Each iteration of magic-wielder was on their own dealing with miscreants.

I was getting way, way ahead of the curve. I might go sleuthing and find nothing.

Or I might end up so far over my head, I slunk back to Faery to beg reinforcements. It would be an uphill battle. My people are loathe to involve themselves in non-Fae affairs, but the world was changing.

Question was, would it change in time to suit my current needs.

Morning didn't bring further clarity.

After washing my face in the sink in my room, I got into my work clothes. We start early, well before breakfast at the lodging. As I'd done many mornings, I showed up for roll call, worked a couple of hours, and journeyed back to the house for food.

I'm adept at covering my tracks. No one's ever discovered I actually leave the jobsite entirely—unless I want them to.

Breakfast was well underway. I filled a plate and sat at an empty table. Where was Morgan? I'd expected her to join me, but a trip into the kitchen to check on her would surely engender notice.

I ate slowly. Refilled my coffee cup. I'd almost decided to drop in on Zeke to figure out what had happened when

Morgan ducked through the swinging door leading to the kitchen with a plate in her hands.

Offering a warm smile, she dropped into a chair opposite me. "Sorry. I was caught up with pre-lunch preparations. Who knew what a production number it would be to cook without mag— Oops."

"It's okay. I get it. Did you sleep well?"

She nodded. "Took a while to fall asleep. Zeke and I were out early for his walk, and I've been working in the kitchen since seven. Looks as if you've been at work too."

"What tipped you off?" I smiled back. Being with her was such a joy, my mind and body brimmed with anticipation. I reined it in. We were slowly becoming friends. If I pushed for more, she'd run the other way.

"Maybe the hard hat on the floor next to you?" She took a few more bites of breakfast and lowered her voice. "On a more serious note, Zeke and I are going to the place I last, erm, talked with Mother."

"Sure you want to do that alone?"

"We'll be fine. No one knows about that spot."

"If it's true, then how'd you find out about it?" I set my fork down.

She shrugged, clearly uncomfortable with me grilling her. "Actually, other sisters showed me, but it was long ago."

Crap. This was getting worse and worse. *"How do you know they won't be lying in wait for you?"* I switched to mind speech.

"They weren't last time. Besides, Zeke will be there."

"Can't you wait until I'm off work?" I didn't want to risk raising my voice. The dining room was roughly half full of other residents.

"I thought we were going to go see your associate then."

She'd quit eating too. Damn it. I was coming off like a heavy-handed asshole. Making a grab for my temper, I said, "Yes, I will set that up."

"Good. I'll see you this evening." Pushing her chair back, she started to leave.

"Morgan. Please."

Something in my voice must have drilled through. She sank into her chair. "Do you know something you haven't told me?"

"No. Not exactly."

"Then what is it?"

"There's more to this than what's on the surface. Until we know more, it's not safe for you to go digging around on your own."

"I've been digging around all my life—by myself."

"I'm not asking you not to do it, just to wait till I can be there."

Lines formed in her forehead; she pressed her lips together. *"What about Mother? She said she's all right, but they imprisoned her. How 'all right' does that sound to you?"*

"If you're going to try to rescue your mother, all the more reason to bring me along."

"Maybe so." She reverted to a normal conversational tone.

"Then you'll wait?"

"I can't make any promises. I need to go back to the kitchen. Piles of dishes are waiting."

It was all I was going to get. I couldn't treat her like a child. She wasn't one, and it would be disrespectful.

The sway of her hips as she walked away was alluring, but worry overshadowed lust. I hastily finished my food.

I'd return to the jobsite, come up with an excuse, and leave for the remainder of the day. Whether I'd let Morgan know I was shadowing her remained to be seen.

At least she wouldn't be alone.

Zeke would know I was close, but he was my buddy.

Perhaps I'd be aboveboard and be waiting when she launched a spell to leave. Sensing such things is well within my scope. So is jumping into a fledgling spell and sharing its magic.

Of course, I've never tried it with a witch before, but how hard could it be?

CHAPTER ELEVEN, MORGAN

Damien's attitude was worrisome. Had I made a mistake letting him into my life? No one's told me what to do—or forbade me from acting as I saw fit—since before Mother quit hiding my eyes.

Back in the kitchen, I placed my dirty plate on top of a stack of others and retrieved my apron, tying it behind me. The cook sat on a tall stool writing in a notebook. When he was done, he ripped out the page and handed it to me.

"Here's what we need for lunch and dinner. Smythe has an account at Green's Market. When you've finished the dishes, go shopping."

I stared at the list, flummoxed. I've never shopped for groceries in my life. Someone else in the Coven had borne that responsibility. Everything on the list was recognizable, so if I went into this Green's Market, I could probably locate the items.

"Something wrong?" The cook eyed me.

I shook my head. "Where is the store?"

"Oh. That's right. You haven't been here long. It's two blocks away at the corner of Hill and Third Avenue. You can wheel the cart back here so long as you return it."

So much for my leisurely morning returning to the place Mother had connected with me.

I read through the list again, in case something wasn't clear, before stuffing it into a pocket.

"Shop carefully," he told me. "Buy what's on sale if you can."

"Got it." Turning away, I went to work on the dishes. "How will the store clerk know I'm from here?"

"What was that?" He looked up from chopping celery.

I repeated myself, but louder.

"Mmph. Good point. Hold on." After he'd rinsed and dried his hands, he retrieved the notebook and a pen. He scratched something out and handed the note to me.

"Put it someplace dry," I said not willing to interrupt my task. I'd only been at this for a couple of days, but I already hated doing dishes. The sooner I finished, the better.

I was hanging up my damp towel and untying my apron when the cook cleared his throat. "None of my affair, but what's up with your eyes?"

Heat rose from the neck of my shirt. I looked away,

thought fast, and came up with what I hoped was a credible lie. "The white one is blind."

"Poor thing."

"Don't need your pity," I mumbled. Gaze still downcast, I snatched the note and tucked it away with the grocery list.

"I suppose not. Well, you'll be safe here. Not all these places are good for young women, if you catch my drift."

I did. "Thanks for your concern, but I have Zeke."

"Oh yeah, the dog. He can hang out in the kitchen while you work if you'd like."

My smile was heartfelt. "Thank you. He'd love it. Being cooped up in the room by himself is hard."

"Where were you before you came here?"

Oh-oh.

I should have come up with a credible backstory. Would have if I'd known I needed one.

When I didn't answer, he patted my shoulder. "It's okay. I understand. Get going with those groceries, eh? I need some of that stuff for lunch."

"Will do." I walked out of the kitchen intent on grabbing Zeke. I had no idea if he'd be welcome in a food market. If not, I could tie him to something outside the door.

What on earth did the cook think my history entailed? That I was fresh out of prison? Or I'd escaped an evil pimp? Regardless, he hadn't pressed the issue.

Locating the store was simple. It was far larger than

I'd imagined. A sign on the front door said the only dogs allowed were service animals. Zeke didn't seem to fit into that category, so he lay next to a bicycle rack with a faux lead securing him to it.

With the list clutched firmly in one hand, I ventured into the store. Everyone seemed to have a cart, so the first thing I did was locate a passel of them. Luckily, the place was well organized. All the fruit and vegetables were in one spot. I did my best to buy the cheapest items I could while gazing longingly at plump, succulent organic berries and oranges.

My next stop was at a deli counter for equally cheap sliced meat and cheese. Potatoes, corned beef hash, tinned tuna, and white bread completed the items I'd been sent for. Taking a chance, I located the drug store aisle and bought a dollar toothbrush and a small tube of toothpaste.

In for a penny, in for a pound, I dropped a hairbrush into the cart too.

The check stand was nip and tuck. I gave a young man the letter from the cook. He had to call someone else who took their sweet time showing up to verify I could leave the store with my items.

Meanwhile, the line behind me grew longer and longer with restive people muttering and cursing. I tossed a calming spell over my shoulders instructing it to encompass the entire line. They quieted immediately.

Soon, I was on my way with Zeke trotting next to me

as I pushed the cart toward our lodging house. When I went around by the kitchen door, the cook opened it as if he'd been waiting for me.

Maybe he had. For all he knew, I'd fill my own larder courtesy of his letter allowing me to purchase on their dime. Had I done that, I'd have vanished. He'd taken a chance on me, and I was grateful for his trust.

Once the bags had been off loaded, I said, "I bought a couple of things for myself. Tell me how much I owe, and I'll pay as soon as I have some money."

The cook frowned. "You weren't supposed to stray from the list."

"I'm sorry. I bought a toothbrush, toothpaste, and a hairbrush. That's all. It's not like I tried to hide it from you."

His frown deepened. "You don't have a toothbrush?"

I shook my head.

He patted my shoulder and rummaged through the bags laying my things aside. "Don't worry about it. Return the cart. Collect these items after you come back."

"I want to pay for them," I insisted. "But Smythe doesn't pay me. I'm going to work on getting a job that does. When I do, I'll be good for those few dollars."

He didn't respond, so I traipsed back to the market with Zeke and slotted the cart into an outside rack. Shopping hadn't been as hard as I'd feared. And the cook —Charles—hadn't been angry about my extra purchases.

"He sees you as a daughter," Zeke observed.

"But how? He barely knows me."

"Doesn't matter. Don't fight it. His soft spot toward you will work in your favor."

I patted his head. "And yours. He said you can hang out in the kitchen while I work."

"Scraps?" Zeke woofed hopefully.

"Probably not. Most of that food is marginal."

"You're eating it."

"Because I have to keep up my strength."

Until my trip through the market, I hadn't realized the food at the Coven was top notch. Neither had I understood items of lesser value were readily available.

The cook wasn't there when I retrieved my purchases and walked upstairs to my room. After leaving Zeke, I stopped by the bathroom to brush my teeth and tease out my tangled locks. It took longer than I'd anticipated. I also needed soap and shampoo of my own, but one thing at a time.

When I returned, Zeke had his paws on the window ledge staring outside. After jumping down, he turned to me. *"Are we still going to the hills to find Zoelle?"*

I glanced at a clock mounted on the wall. It was only nine thirty. "Sure. We have time before I'm due in the kitchen for lunch prep at eleven."

"Are you sure?" His nostrils flared. *"Might be best to wait until you're done with lunch. We'd have more time."*

A light tap on my door sent me flying to open it. I should have checked who was there, but if it had been one of my erstwhile sisters, I'd have sensed their magic. Furthermore, Zeke would have warned me.

It wasn't as if the Coven was about to hunt me down. They'd made their choice.

The cook stood in my doorway. "Thought maybe you could use these." He thrust a small box of laundry detergent and a stack of quarters into my hand. "Laundry's in the basement."

Before I could stammer my thanks, he was gone.

Suddenly, Zeke's idea to push our trip to find Mother to later in the day made sense. All I needed was something to wear while I washed my few clothes. I could raid Damien's closet.

Except I did not want to be beholden to him.

After dithering back and forth for a few minutes, I walked along the hall to his room and knocked. I hadn't expected him to answer. When he didn't, I let myself in with magic and promises to tell him exactly what I'd done and why.

His spicy, alluring scent surrounded me. The temptation to snoop was strong. I ignored it, snatched a robe off a hook, and left, making certain the door was locked behind me.

The laundry machines were huge, so large I opted to wash my garments out in a sink and spin them in a centrifuge. Luckily, we'd had one at the guild house, so I understood how to operate it. Once most of the moisture was gone, I spent one of my precious quarters in a dryer.

Garbed in clothes that didn't stink of days-old sweat, I returned Damien's robe and made it to the kitchen in good time for lunch preparation. Zeke curled up in a corner, making himself unobtrusive. From time to time, the cook tossed him a hunk of something. No matter what it was, Zeke woofed thanks, his tail thumping the floor.

"READY TO LEAVE?" I asked the wolf. We were back in our room so I could grab my coat. I couldn't afford to waste magic keeping warm. Who knew what we'd find where we were headed?

He jumped on me, paws on my shoulders, and licked my face. He'd always loved Mother. Her hawk and he were fast friends. I hadn't thought about it until now, but he must miss her.

And I missed Coven life even if I didn't miss any individual witches—not after the stunt they'd pulled. I'd been comfortable there, never imagining they'd dismiss me summarily.

Had not even a single witch stood up for me?

Mother had answers. Whether she'd share them remained to be seen.

After visualizing my destination, I drew the necessary elements into a travel spell. Simpler to leave from here. While it hadn't been raining when I'd gone to the market, it was now. Maybe we'd get lucky and the spot north of town would host a patch of clear weather. The walls of my room developed a liquid aspect before swirling to nothing. In their place, rolling green hills took shape. Since I'd never run into anyone here, I didn't bother shaping magic to ward us.

Rain still fell, but lightly. I tugged my hood over my head. Zeke took off at a run. I squelched through wet grass enjoying air not tainted by automobile exhaust. As I walked, I called for Mother, opening my mind voice to its widest extent.

She didn't answer.

At first, I kept trying, but after a while worry carved a track through me. What had the Coven done with her? Had they found out she'd connected with me and taken steps to ensure it never happened again?

My hands curled into fists. Damn it. I refused to let the few witches in charge separate me from my only blood kin.

What can I do about it? an inner voice groused.

Good question. Surely, I could come up with something. Preferably a solution not reliant on Damien and the Fae. It seemed they were willing to help. Meant they knew something just like Mother did. Unlikely they'd involve themselves with another iteration of magic-wielder unless the need was great.

Zeke loped to where I was, ears pricked forward. *"Have you caught so much as a glimmer?"*

I shook my head.

"We cannot give up."

"We're going to have to. Pretty soon, we'll have to return. The cook has been kind to us. I don't want to let him down."

Zeke plopped on his haunches, threw his head back, and howled, long, low, mournful. The sound was so sad, it cut me to my bones.

Wingbeats drew my attention to the skies. I shielded my eyes with my hands and then checked with magic. Zeke was still howling. I placed a hand on his head.

"That's Mother's bird."

Zeke stopped mid-howl and switched to excited yips.

Sita swooped in and landed on my shoulders, talons digging in hard enough to cause pain. Mother may have been only partially present, but Sita was 100 percent here.

"You must help," the bird chirped.

"Tell us everything." Zeke was on his feet.

"No time." The hawk sounded frantic, beak clacking in triple time.

I reached into her mind, but it was closed to me. Alarm bells tolled. Yes, it was Mother's familiar, but I couldn't afford any errors about why she was here.

"You must provide details. I am but one witch. Diving into a situation where Zeke and I are outmatched isn't wise."

"But it's your mother," Sita insisted.

"Then, why is your mind a blank?" There, I'd said it.

The hawk spread her wings, but I was faster. After

looping a magical net around her, I pried her off my shoulders and hung on. "You will tell us everything, or we're not going anywhere."

Zeke nudged me, whining. *"You're being harsh. This is Sita, my friend."*

Breath hissed through clenched teeth. "Maybe I am, but I can't see into her mind. The Coven might be using her to lure us into a trap."

I raised the bird to eye level, intent on boring a hole through her defenses.

A shot of magic jolted me. For a second I feared it had come through the bird in my hands.

Damien loped through a pale-green gateway, fair hair floating around his shoulders. "Be pissed later. For now, let me help you."

Zeke barked, hackles at half-mast. For once, he didn't run to the Fae.

I stood frozen in place unsure what to do. Something was off with Sita. If Damien could chop through the mystery, maybe I should accept his help. Blended magic is always stronger.

"Good idea." He hustled to my side.

"What's a good idea?" I sent a pointed glance skittering his way.

"Blending our magic to determine what's going on."

"Fuck this. Stay out of my head."

"And out of your spells?" He smiled, engaging as ever.

Oh yeah. Must be how he'd tracked me.

I should be furious, kick his ass out of the glade.

"Like I said, be pissed later. Let's peel enough layers to see more clearly."

Zeke's hackles wilted. He walked to Damien and nudged him in the ribs. *"Can you help my friend?"*

"If your bondmate allows it." He scratched between the wolf's ears.

Both of them stared at me. Sita wriggled in my grip, but I wasn't about to let her go. I tightened the weave of the magical net I'd snared her with.

"All right," I said at length. "Let's do this."

Zeke yipped.

Damien said, "Thanks for trusting me. Must be hard after what happened to you."

"You have no idea."

"Probably not." Laying a hand over one of mine, he joined the spell holding Sita.

Because I could, I adopted a dual view, through my eyes and his. "Holy shit," I mumbled and nearly dropped the bird.

"Not what I expected," Damien gritted.

"Tell me," Zeke demanded, every bit of fur standing on end.

"You may as well kill me," Sita croaked, not bothering with telepathy. Unlike Zeke, her vocal cords allowed understandable speech. "I cannot go back. Not now."

CHAPTER TWELVE, DAMIEN

I returned to the lodging in time to see Morgan and Zeke go shopping. The foreman had not been pleased when I said I was coming down with something and needed to go home. He'd skirted within an inch of telling me to clock out permanently. And he would have were he not so short staffed. Skilled workmen had their pick of jobs. Mine was far from the best-paying worksite, but it allowed me latitude to take the occasional sick day.

I kept watch while Morgan washed clothes after she helped herself to one of my bathrobes.

Shameless of me, but catching glimpses of her body was too tantalizing to walk away from. Not as if I leered at her the whole time. I made myself scarce after full, round breasts with copper-brown nipples gave me a hell of a hard-on.

I should get a life. Couldn't recall the last time I'd bedded a woman. How pathetic is that? My Dark Fae cousins are another matter entirely. Sex is a centerpiece of their existence. We've always looked down our noses at their extensive rutting, but some of us—me, for instance—were secretly jealous.

The lunch hour dragged. I was hungry, so I snagged a couple of sandwiches when no one was looking. Not that they'd have seen me, but they'd have seen food move off the serving platter, hover for a moment, and disappear into thin air.

I was killing time, holding an invisibility illusion and waiting. No wonder my mind chased one tangent after another. At least my errant member wasn't doing its flagpole imitation.

Finally, Morgan cobbled a journey spell together. I'd been afraid she'd notice me, but my caution paid off. She had no idea I'd tracked her until I strode from my own portal.

The shit didn't exactly hit the fan. She could have told me to get lost. It would have put me in a tough spot. Not much hope of blending magic or much of anything else when the other mage isn't willing.

Lucky for me, a familiar had shown up. In theory, it was Morgan's mother's bird. I came in on the tail end of the bird requesting aid and telling Morgan she had to accompany her pronto.

Morgan's instincts urged caution. Good thing. After

she reluctantly accepted my help, I joined magic with hers and blasted through warding wound around the hawk's mind. Witches resided there, many of them. They scattered like leaves in a staunch wind the moment they sensed my presence.

A sharp yip from Zeke said he was waiting to hear what we'd discovered. "She's been turned into a conduit," I told him. "Witches took over her mind—and her will."

Rearing on his haunches, Zeke licked the hawk still balanced in Morgan's hands. She made sad little cooing sounds.

Furrows formed between Morgan's dark brows. "Why did you leave Mother's side?"

"Had to," Sita squawked.

"Why?" I repeated.

"They said they'd hurt her worse if I didn't." The hawk's beak clacked after a mournful cry.

"Is the bond broken forever?" I asked Morgan.

She shook her head. "Not sure. Never ran into this before. Once a familiar and a witch pledge to one another, it's always been permanent."

Morgan directed her gaze at Sita. "What does Mother know?"

"Many things."

She shook the bird. "Do better."

"Or what?" Another beak clack.

"I'll send you to the Fae dungeons," I told her.

She rustled her feathers. "You cannot hurt me worse

than I already have been. My heart, my life is lost to me. They've been watching this glade. As soon as they sensed you here, they sent me."

"To do what?" Morgan growled.

"Get you to come with me."

"Where would we have been going?" I cut in.

"Somewhere the Coven could capture me," Morgan muttered. "Guess they decided cutting me loose was a mistake."

All fine and well, but they hadn't counted on my presence. The witches piloting the hawk may have scattered, but eyes were on us. They knew I was here. It complicated matters. They had no idea I'd eavesdropped on their conversation about Morgan being some kind of universal queen.

Fae power is weak enough, they'd probably discount my presence, consider me collateral damage.

If they made a move.

"Damien?"

"Yeah."

"Your mind is busy, but I can't interrupt the spell I'm holding Sita with to look deeper."

Thank the goddess for small favors.

"Where is Morgan's mother?" I sent the question deep into Sita's mind, diving after it. I wasn't leaving until I knew.

After a painful pause where I felt the hawk struggling not to capitulate—and I was damned if I knew why—images tumbled through my mind. Unfamiliar places.

"Do you recognize any of this?" I asked Morgan.

"Yes. It's the old castle not far from our guild house in northern England."

So far, so good. We had a location. Hopefully, not a well-guarded one. "Why is Sita's loyalty with witches other than your mother?"

"Can't answer that."

The hawk went limp in her hands, eyes closing. I had my answer. Witches were indeed still watching. They'd threatened to kill the hawk if she failed in her mission, and she'd revealed far too much.

"Give her to me, quickly." I held out my hands.

Morgan clutched the dying hawk to her breast, stroking soft, reddish feathers.

"Do you have healing magic?" I asked. When she shook her head, I repeated, "Give her to me. Hurry, or it will truly be too late."

Zeke barked and banged his head into Morgan's side.

She dropped the hawk into my hands. Kneeling, I placed Sita on the ground and called on Danu to aid my efforts. Since I'd already been inside the hawk's mind, it was simple enough to clip the threads connecting her to distant witches. Once I got them out of the way, I settled in and repaired damage one vessel at a time.

It took a while. All my attention was on Sita. Zeke and Morgan faced outward with me between them. A destruction spell had been cunningly woven around Sita's heart, moving from there to her hollow bones. The casting did not want to die. Every time I thought I'd defeated it, it bounced back.

Sweat beaded my forehead. Should I teleport back to Faery for one of our healers? They're far more skilled than me. The hawk quivered beneath my ministrations. It decided me. I'd lose her if I returned her to Faery; the transport would finish the job.

Time dribbled past, a lot of it. So much, the sun was heading for the western horizon by the time I allowed myself to hope I'd won. The hawk's heartbeat was steady. No witch taint remained in her small, feathered body.

"How is she?" Morgan was still turned away, scanning for any alterations that would signal we were under attack.

"Stable. We can leave."

Zeke howled but cut it off midstream. *"We have to go now."*

I felt witch taint—not clean like Morgan's but compromised in some unknown way—the moment he said we needed to leave.

Guess they'd felt me sever their spell and were riding in to sow chaos.

Morgan was ready with travel magic. No doubt, she'd crafted it, holding it in abeyance for just this eventuality. My appreciation for her, already high, notched upward as her magic swept us away. It would have taken me time to switch from full-on healing to teleporting.

"I picked your room," she said.

"It's fine. Sita will need a spot to recuperate, and I'll make certain she's delivered to our healers in Faery."

"*Thank you,*" the hawk croaked.

Morgan stroked her head. "Mother would never forgive me if something happened to you."

"*Will I ever see her again?*" Every feather drooped.

"If I have anything to say about it, you will," Morgan promised.

"Bet they won't keep her at that place in England," I ventured. Healing magic still burned a path through me. Not so simple to turn off when I was done with it.

"It will take them time to move her," Morgan said. "Means we have to act quickly. Tonight after dinner."

"*You have to take me.*" Sita rolled in my hands until her feet were under her.

"The best place for you is with Fae healers," I told the hawk.

"I agree with him," Morgan said. "Even if we manage to beat the Coven to where Mother is sequestered, it will be close. And dangerous. You won't have your full strength for quite some time."

"*I still want to go,*" Sita croaked.

"*You would be our weakest link,*" Zeke told her. "*Our goal is to locate Zoelle and bring her back. As soon as she's here, we'll bring you to her.*"

"*Our bond will require renewal.*" The bird sounded despondent.

"Mother would do anything to keep you in her life," Morgan said.

Something about her words must have reassured the hawk because she quieted. As we waited out the spell, I hatched up my next moves. I'd bring Sita to Faery. While I was there, I'd do what I could to scare up a couple more Fae to accompany us to England.

Anyone who'd witnessed Maeve's peek into the Coven's inner machinations should be eager to go. We don't involve ourselves with other iterations of mage, but we do step in when evil is at play.

I had no way to be positive, but I'd bet damn near anything Morgan's old Coven was knee-deep in a hell-spawned deal with darkness.

As soon as we got back, Morgan and Zeke hightailed it for the kitchen. They were only a few minutes late, but the cook had been kind to Morgan and she didn't want him to regret taking her under his wing.

I gave it a few minutes to ensure we hadn't been followed. While Morgan manipulated the journey spell, I'd kept a close eye for taggers on. I'd just been one, so I knew what to look for.

Sita perched on the edge of a table, looking a bit the

worse for wear. *I've never been to Faery. Will I be a prisoner?"*

"Of course not. You will be free to leave at any time." I paused for emphasis. "The Coven will be looking for you. They cannot penetrate Faery's borders, so it's the safest spot for you at the moment."

If was half a white lie. Any determined mage could blast their way into Faery, but Sita needed peace. Worry would impede her recovery. Besides, I didn't think the witches would engage all of Faery in an out-and-out war over one familiar.

"Why would you do this for me?" Sita angled her head to one side and nailed me with her lidless avian gaze.

"Morgan is important to me. I want to help her as much as I can."

The hawk bobbed her head. *"Zoelle would like you."*

"Thank you. It's quite a compliment."

"You have no idea. She rarely likes anyone inside the Coven or out."

I grinned. Something about the plainspoken hawk drew me in. "Ready to leave?"

The hawk bobbed her head. I crafted a gateway to take us to Faery.

Maeve met us at the point where my portal cleaved Faery's veils. "Took you a while," she commented.

"How'd you know—?" I held up a hand and muttered, "Never mind." Of course the Fae seer would have been keeping an eye on me after my last visit.

"A healer will be here presently, but first"—Maeve switched her attention to Sita—"I have questions. The first is, when did the Coven separate you and Zoelle?"

"Months ago. Long before they made Morgan leave."

"I see." Maeve narrowed her blue eyes. "What have you been doing in the interim?"

Sita clacked her beak. *"Trying to stay out of sight."*

"Didn't work very well, did it?"

The hawk squirmed in my grip; perhaps I'd been holding on too tightly. I let go, and she fluttered to a shoulder. *"You're just like Lilith,"* Sita squawked. *"Always finding fault."*

Laughter rolled from Maeve, so much she bent double before getting hold of herself. "Oh my." She wiped streaming eyes. "I am nothing like the Coven's seer."

Since Sita wasn't offering anything in particular, I said, "What happened after the Coven forced you and Zoelle apart?"

"At first, they kept her in quarters beneath the guild house. I snatched two visits. The second time, they caught me and changed the magical shielding around Zoelle. I couldn't penetrate it."

A warbling sigh was followed by more beak clacking. *"I went to some of the other familiars, the ones I'd been friends with. They wanted to help, but they were frightened. So were their bondmates. In the end, a few brave animals stood by me.*

"They were stunned by Morgan being forced out. In all the years of the Coven, it was a first."

"When did they move Zoelle to England?" I prodded.

"After she contacted Morgan, they must have decided she was too close. So several sisters cast a joint spell to harness enough power to cross the sea."

"How do you know where they took her?" Maeve asked.

"I overheard them."

"How does it jive with lying low and not attracting attention?" Power flickered from Maeve's fingertips, dancing around the hawk.

"I had help from some of the familiars. We formed a spy circle. The sisters found out. It's how they nabbed me and forced me to approach Morgan."

Sita pecked the side of my head gently. *"They hadn't counted on you."*

"Uh-uh." I twisted to glance at Sita. "Give Morgan credit. She didn't fall for your story. When she couldn't see into your mind, she suspected something was amiss."

"Zeke believed me."

"Why would you be party to a plot that would cause harm to Zoelle's daughter?" Maeve asked. The glittering threads oozing from her fingertips wrapped more tightly around Sita.

The hawk hung her head. *"They also captured a cat, a doe, and a rabbit. If I didn't do as they asked, they'd have killed them."*

"Is that common practice?" Maeve's mouth twisted in disgust.

"No, but neither is banishing witches."

The fibers around the bird glowed silver. She'd been truthful with us.

Two healers garbed in traditional white robes sashed in blue trotted close. One held out her hands to Sita. "This must be our patient."

Sita clung to me. I stroked her russet feathers. "Go with them. They will restore your magic."

"Are you angry with me?"

"No. These are unusual times. You were placed in an impossible situation."

Seemingly reassured by my words, Sita jumped into the healer's outstretched hands. She and her companion turned to leave, chanting a soothing melody.

Once they were out of earshot, Maeve turned to me. "I don't care how many witches banded together. Their magic isn't sufficient to cross an ocean."

"Mmph. So they had help."

"Exactly."

It was a good bridge to my next request. I'd been making more than my share of late. "Do you suppose we might scare up a couple of Fae to join Morgan and me?"

"To do what, exactly?"

The corners of my mouth twitched, but I smothered the smile that wanted out. "I assumed you knew since you were up to speed on everything else."

"I don't. Are you going to answer me?"

I nodded. "After today's plan went awry, the Coven will probably move Zoelle."

"Where in northern England is she?"

"A castle on the outskirts of Carlisle. Morgan and I will go there tonight and attempt to free her. If we're lucky, we'll get there ahead of the Coven contingent."

"Coven plus whatever." Maeve stared pointedly, reminding me the witches had help crossing the Atlantic.

"Which makes bringing more Fae along even more essential. Besides, we'll need a critical mass of magic to teleport that far."

"This will set an unusual precedent."

"Hopefully, no one will find out." The words were no sooner out than I realized how naïve they sounded.

"Oh, they'll find out all right." Maeve's eyes were chillier than usual. "Our best hope is this Coven has slid so far off the rails the other ones will disown them."

"Does that mean I can count on assistance?"

"You can't very well follow through without any."

I waited, biting off words before they escaped. I'd said enough. If the Fae wouldn't help, Morgan and I would have a tough go of it on our own. Our magic would be all but tapped out by the time we got to England. We'd have to regroup before converging on Zoelle.

By then, the Coven would have beat us to it, and we'd have to locate her all over again.

"Give me an hour," Maeve said. "I will come with you, but I want to tap Logan and perhaps one more."

"Thank you." I could have hugged our dour seer, but she wouldn't have appreciated it.

"Meanwhile, scuttle back to that subpar place you chose over Faery. Be sure to impress on Morgan she's along for the ride. She must not question our decisions—or our magic."

"Um, her familiar will be with us."

"What does that have to do with her following orders?"

"Nothing." I could have said more but chose not to. Morgan marched to her own drumbeat. She hadn't been a particularly good soldier in the Coven, and I doubted she'd mindlessly follow Fae guidance, either.

"Be there apace."

"Thank you again, Maeve."

"I'm not doing this for you." She settled her hands on her hips. "We are bound to stand against evil. That particular Coven sold out to demons or vamps or some such thing. Let's hope the defection hasn't spread to witches in other locales."

I hadn't even considered the possibility. Perhaps she'd seen something in her glass or her sphere or her pool. No chance to ask; she was already gone.

I retraced my steps through the veils holding Faery separate from Earth and hurried back to the lodging house. Maeve had labeled it subpar. Compared with Faery, she was accurate, but the place held one undeniable appeal.

I could be whomever I wished and not have to answer to anyone.

Yeah, those days are over.

By requesting favors, I'd all but committed myself to returning to the fold fulltime. No more splitting my energy between Earth and Faery.

CHAPTER THIRTEEN, MORGAN

Zeke and I had been waiting for about fifteen minutes when Damien popped through a gateway and into his room. I jumped up from my perch on his bed. "We're ready."

"Patience. A few Fae are coming along, and—"

"What?" Disbelief churned through my guts. Disappointment, too, that he'd discussed our mission with anyone. "This is our project. Ours. We don't need anyone except the three of us," I sputtered.

Damien crossed to where I stood. "Do you have sufficient magic to cross an ocean via teleporting?"

"Um, no, but you must."

"Really? And you know all about Fae enchantment?"

My cheeks heated; I floundered, hunting for a snappy rejoinder and not coming up with much. "You're saying we need more Fae to even get there? Why didn't you mention that earlier when we were in the glade?"

He was so close, he stole all the air in the room. Made it tough to hang onto my outrage.

"I was swept up in the moment," he explained. "More Fae aren't essential. I command sufficient magic to get us to England. Barely. Once there, I'd have to rest and recuperate for at least a day."

"By then the witches would have moved Mother again." I forced myself to stop talking, since the scope of the problem was clearer.

"Maybe. The consensus in Faery is no matter how many witches banded together, they wouldn't be able to teleport across the Atlantic."

I swallowed hard. I'd known that. After all, we'd had to hire a boat when we'd moved from the Old Country to America. "So, they really are in league with, with something bad?"

"All signs point that way, yes."

I'd known that too, but it hurt my heart. Never mind they'd treated me like yesterday's garbage.

Zeke woofed and walked to my side, offering moral support.

"How many Fae?" I asked doing my damnedest to switch gears and warm to the idea.

"Two or three."

At least it wasn't an entire army. "Will they stay out of the way unless we need them?"

Damien snorted. "Funny, they said the same thing about you."

"But this is my idea. My project. My mother for Hecate's sake."

Breath swooshed from him. "We are all on the same page about the necessity of rescuing Zoelle. Best if we keep that front and center."

"Why? Witches aren't anything to Fae."

"We made a commitment to stand firm against dark magic. It's the only reason my kinsmen agreed to be part of this."

Before I could lodge a protest—although I had no fucking idea what argument I'd launch—he continued. "Let's try to get along. Keep your eye on the ball, Morgan. Getting your mother back is critical. She knows why the Coven blackballed you.

"It's information you'll need as you move forward."

My earlier anger was ceding to resignation. I wasn't pleased with the turn of events, but even I wasn't pigheaded enough not to recognize why Damien had solicited aid.

"Wish you'd have said something," I muttered.

"I am. Now."

"I meant before."

The same gateway he'd used took on a golden glow. Two Fae stepped through, a man and a woman. Both were tall, slender, and swathed in black robes sashed in gold. They looked more like my idea of the Faery-folk. Fair hair had been braided tightly against the man's shapely skull. Silver eyes gleamed from beneath blond brows. The woman had white hair and piercing blue eyes. Something about her felt familiar.

It took a moment before what I sensed clicked into place. She was a seer same as Lilith.

The woman stepped forward. I felt the kiss of her magic as she examined Zeke and me. "At least they didn't sully you before they kicked you out," she said.

I snorted. "Nice to meet you too."

An unexpected smile split her lips. "You have spunk. Excellent. You'll need every scrap before this is through. I am Maeve." She extended a hand.

I grasped it; more magic coursed through me. "This is Zeke," I said, "and I am Morgan, but I suspect you already knew as much."

"I did." The seer knelt in front of Zeke, gazing into his mismatched eyes. He held still beneath her scrutiny.

The wolf licked her face. She crooned to him in Gaelic, a language I'd all but forgotten.

"Hate to break up this love fest"—the male Fae moved closer—"but we need to get moving. I am Logan, head of the Fae council."

I inclined my head to mask my surprise I'd rated such highly placed Fae. Perhaps they had more than one seer, but I doubted it. Lilith wouldn't have tolerated competition.

I'd toyed with leaving a note for the cook letting him know I might not be here tomorrow. In the end, I'd decided not to. If I was MIA, it would probably be for more than a single day. I didn't want to get caught up in lying, and I'd have had to come up with a credible reason I was absent.

Better to mend that bridge later—if it came to it.

"We're ready," I told Logan.

He stood straighter. "Do not fight our magic. At times it won't be comfortable. This is one of many reasons differing iterations of magic-wielders don't work together."

"Got it," I said, anxious to get the next part over with. Once we were at the castle, I'd be closer to my comfort zone.

Damien hooked an arm through mine and motioned to Zeke. Together, we walked through the portal with Logan and Maeve bringing up the rear. I'd traveled with Damien before, but this was different.

Magic prickled the length of my body. It burned and stung by turns. I leaned into Damien and focused on what we'd find at the other end.

He must have been eavesdropping on my thoughts because he said, "Be prepared for anything. Your mother's been tortured—"

"They'd never have done that to her," I protested.

"You can't know. Look what they did to you. All I'm saying is she might not be the witch you remember. It could take time—perhaps quite a bit—and a stint with our healers to bring her around."

"We have our own healers," I began and shut up. They'd never lift a charm to help her, not the way things stood with the Coven.

Discomfort from the journey spell was letting up. Either I'd adapted or the enchantment was changing.

Damien tightened his grip on me. "We're nearly there. It's quite a jolt when we break through."

"Already? We just left." Maybe I'd make it back in time for my kitchen stint after all.

"Time doesn't mean much in Fae spells."

If my body had slammed into a brick wall, I would have had about the same experience. Breath whooshed from me. I didn't scream, but I wanted to. Damien hadn't been kidding about a jolt.

Night spread around us. Well warded, we stood outside a gated stone manor house dating back to the 1500s. The Coven had spelled it before we left to keep mortals from moving in. Appeared the magic had held fast even after centuries passed. Or maybe they'd shored it up when they'd dumped Mother here.

Maeve came up behind me. "Your magic protects this place. You must find us a way through."

I bit back a snarky comment about them realizing I was more than dead weight along for the ride. They'd gone out on a limb to help me. Damien had been right about me not throwing their kindness in their faces. Not that I wanted to. They were here to help. I don't switch gears easily, and the addition of two more Fae had blindsided me.

"Sure," I told her. "Give me a moment. I wasn't the one who crafted this casting, but it doesn't mean I can't unravel it."

With Zeke trotting by my side, his nostrils twitching, I circled the compound. Zeke rattled off names of the witches who'd been involved in the protection spell. I could have figured it out on my own, but his nose was sharper than my magic sometimes.

He wanted to be helpful. Hard to fault him for it.

I took my time, testing each strand woven around the manor house for booby traps. We witches are famous for instilling them into our long-term castings. It lets us know if they've been disturbed. When I found them, I dismantled them in such a way no one would be the wiser.

"*What are you doing?*" Maeve's voice drifted through my mind.

"*Making sure we don't alert anyone. Almost done.*" And I was. After a final check, I returned to the group and led them to a hole I'd crafted toward the back of the structure.

We ducked through. Fae enchantment snugged around me as someone adjusted our warding. I hadn't been particularly careful with it while I'd been working. Didn't seem to have cost us.

Logan held up a hand. We stood behind him while he scanned the area. The annoyance I'd booted into the backseat roared out of hiding. He was looking for Mother. I should be doing that. I'd know her emanations anywhere.

Damien gripped my upper arm. *"They might be expecting you. We're the last type of mage they'd set beacons for."*

"Stay out of my head." I tried to jerk free, but he held fast.

Not the time to get into a pissing match by pointing out the Coven had identified Fae in the glade where they'd sent Sita. Zeke nuzzled my hand. I quieted all the pesky demons that could sabotage our position. So what if the Fae were trampling over my ego; they weren't doing it on purpose.

"Look there." Logan's words were attached to a vector.

I did. And then I opened all my psychic senses and examined the spot he'd indicated again. *"Not sure,"* I murmured. *"Parts are like her; parts are not."*

Maeve took hold of my other arm and spoke into my ear. "Be strong. She may be very changed from your memories."

"You can fix her, right?" I looked into the seer's blue eyes.

"Maybe. Depends on what's wrong."

I winced, grateful she was being honest with me no matter how daunting the message.

Logan moved silently. Maeve and Damien let go of me, and I fell into line behind him, feelers activated as I sought the only true friend I'd ever had. If the Coven had damaged Mother, I'd burn down the world avenging her. Even if it took me a hundred years, I'd hunt down every witch who'd had a part in harming my blood. When I found them, I'd scar them, make them pay for their sins, for whatever bargain they'd forged with dark magic.

We entered the manor house through a side door near the kitchens. Rust coated its hinges, but Logan must have silenced it because it didn't creak. It cost me to admit this, but I was grateful for both him and Maeve. Fae are warriors; witches win through cunning rather than force. The thought jarred me.

"Keep your eyes open for beacons," I told Logan.

He spun and faced me in a long hallway bisecting the manor house. *"What do they look like?"*

"It's more what they feel like. Fire mixed with earth sizzles."

He thrust me ahead. *"You go first."*

This time, I didn't gloat. The stakes were too high. With Zeke padding silently next to me, I covered familiar ground, plucking and dismantling beacons as they cleaved our path. Good thing I'd thought to be alert for them. There'd been so many in the weave around the place, it surprised me the Coven had planted still more.

I examined the next one more closely.

It was recent compared with the ones I'd knocked down outside.

Logan pushed ahead. *"I know what to look for now,"* he said.

The central hall ended; we went down several sets of stairs to a subterranean level that had once held a wine cellar and dungeons. I'd never been below the main floor before. My sense of Mother expanded as we drew closer to her.

My earlier impressions didn't change. It was her, but not. What had the Coven done?

The stairs ended abruptly in a dimly lit corridor. I pitched into Logan. He'd halted, and I'd been stewing in thoughts of revenge.

"What?" I asked softly.

"Something else is here. Wait." He motioned to Maeve and Damien. Zeke and I edged into the circle. We were all in this together. If they were laying plans, we should know what they were.

I didn't have any trouble tapping into their telepathy, but it was in Gaelic. Once I was fluent, but I hadn't heard it spoken in a long while. Because I had to, I added magic to interpret.

And wished I hadn't.

According to Logan, two or three Banshees led by a Dearg Due guarded Mother. People have said Banshees are related to witches. They're not. The irony is they're a type of faery and far more closely linked to the Fae than witches. The Dearg Due was another matter entirely. A female demon, legend had it she roamed the countryside luring unsuspecting men to their deaths.

The Fae had switched to English, perhaps at Damien's request, as they mapped out a strategy.

"We can handle the Banshees," Maeve said. *"They must obey our commands."*

"Are you certain of that?" Damien asked. *"Appears they're linked to the Dearg Due."*

"Aye, quite certain," Maeve replied.

Logan pointed at Damien. *"We will subdue the Dearg Due. The women will free Zoelle and leave."*

"I am not leaving you here with the Dearg," Maeve said.

"No choice," Logan told her. *"It's an order. We will regroup back in Faery.*

"Turn Zoelle over to the healers immediately," he added.

"As if I wouldn't have done it anyway," Maeve muttered.

We stormed down the corridor. No one had mapped out roles for Zeke or I. Meant we could wing it. Why was Maeve so unsure about leaving the men with the demon? I culled through my memory but couldn't come up with a single fact beyond her luring mortal men to their deaths. Should mean the Fae were safe from her mesmerism.

Should.

A shiver slithered down my spine. Damien had volunteered to help me; so had Logan and Maeve. I sent a prayer winging toward Hecate to watch over them, even though they weren't witches. She's the only goddess I know, the only one I have faith in.

Logan hesitated for a beat in front of the ironclad door that led to the dungeons. Lightning forked from his outstretched hand.

The door burst open. We leapt through.

The first thing to hit me was the smell of decayed flesh, sickly sweet and revolting. Mother huddled in a corner with her arms wrapped around her knees. Flesh sloughed off her in putrescent hunks. She'd pulled out most of her hair. It piled on the floor around her as if she'd tried to create a nest.

The sharp stench of urine and feces mingled with rot as she sat in her own waste.

The Banshees looked like Fae who'd fallen on hard times with bony chins, matted hair, and gaunt bodies. They were naked, wrinkled flesh sinking in on itself. One opened her mouth, but before the traditional shriek could emerge, Maeve raised both hands.

"Silence until I say different."

The Banshees shrank back, but Mother's third guardsperson, the Dearg, leapt to her feet. Contrasting with the Banshees, she was beautiful in a way that made it tough to drag my gaze away. Flame-red curls spilled down her shoulders. An emerald-green gown showcased alabaster skin. Her breasts were bare.

Power oozed from her as she glided toward Logan. "Ummm, Fae. Come to me, ye handsome devil."

Logan took one jerky step toward the Dearg.

Maeve jumped between them. Darts flew from her hands, tangling in the Dearg's hair. "You will leave him alone."

Raucous laughter shook the dungeon. When the Dearg's mouth was open, it showcased double rows of razor-sharp teeth.

Damn. She's like a dragon.

The thought jolted me into action. I ran to Mother. Zeke was already there, licking her face and arms. Her green eyes fluttered open and then went wide. "Oh no. They'll get you too. You shouldn't have come. I told you not to. Told you. Told you. Told you."

Her eyes glazed over and turned vacant as she checked out. Everyone else was engaged, so I gathered Mother into my arms, set a spell in motion, and left the dungeon. Aiming for somewhere outside the warding around the manor house, I mostly succeeded. I could still see the place, but it was a good half a kilometer away.

"Where do we go from here?" Zeke asked.

Good question. I had no money. My magic couldn't get us home. Mother was unconscious. I could carry her, but her diminished state would probably lead some do-gooder to alert local authorities.

Maeve needed to stay where she was to make certain the men didn't fall prey to the Dearg. I could still feel her hypnotic pull from my vantage point, and it creeped me out. Evil is far more present in the Old Country. I'd lived in the States so long, I'd forgotten about Kelpies and Pookas and the Abhartach. Or the Fear Gorta.

"Found her," Maeve called.

Was really her or some fell creature borrowing her voice—and her energy? I swathed us in layers of invisibility.

"Where?" Logan asked.

"Damn it. She was right here."

"It's them," Zeke woofed.

He's almost always right, but if this were one of the times he wasn't?

"Morgan. Show yourself." Maeve's command was sharp and laced with compulsion.

"Damien is fighting for his life on your account. Do not be a twit," Logan shouted.

Guess the need for stealth was behind us. I inhaled once deeply and jettisoned my ward. Logan and Maeve stood over me.

I started to apologize but changed my mind. I'd be damned if I'd grovel for being careful and protecting my mother.

"You have to leave with Zoelle," Logan said. "I'm going back in there to assist Damien. He was in pretty good shape when I left—"

"Then why isn't he here?" I demanded, hugging Mother closer.

"Dearg's are in a class by themselves," he snarled.

Maeve wrapped her arms around Mother and dragged her upright. "Stay close," she told me. "I have my hands full, and there's only one of me to manipulate the journey spell."

I only had a second, but I made a choice. "Zeke and I will remain here. We'll help Logan free Damien. Mother is safe. I'll see her in Faery."

"Go with Maeve," Logan thundered.

I stood tall, shoulders squared. "No. I'm remaining here. Don't be pigheaded. Zeke and I are handy in a fight. And we can blend our magic with yours. It might make us stronger than the Dearg."

"She has a point," Maeve said, snapped her fingers, and was gone with Mother in her arms.

"Are you always this contrary?" Logan growled.

"You should see me on my bad days. Let's go."

Zeke and I loped after Logan. He didn't cut us any slack, but I didn't expect him to. Besides, Zeke is quicker than anything on two legs. When we burst into the dungeons, Damien was on his back with the Dearg straddling him. Her mouth was open, and she'd aimed it right at his jugular.

"Nooooo," I shrieked and landed on top of her.

Zeke fastened his jaws around her shoulder. The satisfying crunch of bones told me he'd done some real damage. The Dearg squealed; her head rotated at an unnatural angle, and she aimed her still-open mouth at Zeke.

We'd show Logan he hadn't made a mistake including us.

More importantly, we'd rescue Damien. Whatever fuckery the demon had done paralyzed him except for his eyes. I fell into their sparkling depths just before I knocked the Dearg clear across the hardpacked dirt floor with Zeke still clinging to her shoulder.

Logan was knee-deep in Banshees. More had converged on the dungeons, but my attention was squarely on Damien. What in Hecate's name had the Dearg done to him?

CHAPTER FOURTEEN, DAMIEN

One minute Morgan was there, and then she was gone. She must have teleported Zoelle to safety. All fine and well. We'd find her once we'd corralled this group.

Logan and Maeve didn't share my views.

"Where'd the witch go?" Logan shouted, staring into shadows as if he expected her to pop out of one.

"She got her mother out of here," I explained.

"No one told her to go it alone," Maeve growled.

"I'm sure she's waiting for us."

"Of course, she would be," Logan snarked. "She can't get back alone."

Defensive words rose to the fore. Because none of us were paying attention, the Banshees broke loose from Logan's hold on them and jumped him, almost pushing him to his knees.

A containment spell poured from him, filling the fetid space with his rich baritone. It cleaved through their magic, but before they stopped plucking at his clothing, two more oozed through from somewhere.

The Dearg took advantage of the chaos to slither around behind me. I felt the drag of her enchantment slowing me until I swam through molasses. Maeve was saying something, her tone urgent, but I couldn't make it out.

Somehow, I ended up sprawled on my back with the Dearg crawling on top of me. A barrier rose between me and my magic. Spells bounced from one side of my head to the other, but couldn't make it into the light of day.

Or, in this case, the dimly lit subterranean dungeon.

My voice took a hike too. Telepathy was a joke. No magic to send words—or do anything else. Worse, I was losing control of my body. When I tried to throw the Dearg off me, my muscles reacted sluggishly. The warm gentle molasses had shifted to concrete.

Why weren't Logan and Maeve helping?

With the last of my strength, I craned my neck around. Fuck me. I was alone with the Dearg and a rapidly burgeoning population of Banshees.

At least Morgan and her mother had escaped.

If I had any hopes of joining them, I'd have to get myself out of this mess.

Nice goal, but how?

The Dearg had been toying with me. She shouldn't

have been able to hold me in place with just her bodyweight, yet here we were. I couldn't do much beyond blinking my eyelids. Where she ran knobby fingertips down my body, chills followed.

The touch of evil is never pleasant, and she was old beyond measure. Legends surrounding her suggested she rose from the dead one night each year on the anniversary of her suicide to feast on mortal blood.

Except I was scarcely mortal. Was she hoping for more than one day of depraved killing if she branched out from human ichor? I refused to be the instrument adding to her evil.

What could I do?

With naught left to me but thoughts, I called her name, her real one, Orga. Red-rimmed dark eyes zeroed in on me. Aha. Meant she'd heard. Names hold power that extends beyond the grave. If I could buy time, maybe she'd make a mistake, and I'd find a way to break free of this hypnotic trance.

The Banshees had formed a ring around us. I couldn't see the whole of it, but enough to be baffled. Who was calling them? Were some of the Coven close by?

For some reason, the chokehold on telepathy retreated enough for me to communicate. While I had the Dearg's attention, I kept my mind voice soft, soothing, and I spoke in Gaelic, a language she was certain to understand.

"Ye've had a hard time of it, ye wee poor lass. Forced to

wed a man ye dinna love. He treated you horribly, locking you away in a tower for only him to ravish."

"What would ye know of any of that?" she growled displaying fangs stained by blood.

"I am old. Folklore looms large in Faery. 'Tis how we teach our younglings."

Good. She was talking with me. I tested the enchantment circling us, searching for a weak spot.

"What else do ye know?" She went back to stroking my neck and arms. Every place she touched quivered with outrage. I did my best to mask my disgust. Gratitude filled me that Morgan had escaped. By now, the group should be back in Faery and Zoelle ensconced with our healers.

All I had to do was make good on an escape to join them. It wouldn't tax me too badly to transport only myself. I rustled through my magical reservoir checking its level. Nope, not complete enough to allow major spells. Not yet. If I could divert her sufficiently, maybe her focus would shift away from throttling my ability.

"What else do ye know?" she shouted, spraying me with spittle.

"The man who loved you, whom you should have married, Grian, never stopped mourning your death. He never married, and he visited your grave until his own demise."

I tested my bonds again, delighted to find a hole in the weave surrounding me. I ordered a small surge of magic to penetrate not expecting much. When it connected with the break, I'd have crowed if I could have without giving myself away.

"He did not," the Dearg announced. "Ye're lying."

"Fae canna lie." Where was she in the twenty-four hour cycle when she woke each year? Could I ride this out, and she'd vanish on her own?

Nice thought, but unlikely. I might not know how much time remained on the clock, but she did. If I was her prey du jour, she'd never allow herself to get so sidetracked she lost by default.

"Tell me about him, about Grian."

"Do ye not remember him well?" I batted the ball back her way since the only thing I knew was his name and the story of their quashed love. Her father had chosen to wed his daughter to a wealthy noble instead of a poor farrier. Far from an unusual occurrence in those days.

Her gaze lost its sharp edges. She placed both hands on my shoulders and leaned inward. "Not well. The blood that brings me life, erodes my memories. Very little remains."

I checked on the breach. I was making progress, but not enough. At this rate, the hole would be noticeable before it was big enough for me to capitalize on it.

Maybe.

Like many creatures driven by evil, she didn't seem overly smart. Every time she returned to the well for more blood, it gnawed at the few remaining shreds of her humanity.

"Ye will tell me what you know of Grian. I wish to remember him, and I canna." Her fingers tightened on my shoulders. She ran her tongue up my neck. "Ye will tell me while I feed."

Oh-oh. Who in the hell knew what effect her saliva would have on my blood, or my blood on her magical ability. I did not want to find out.

"If ye would hear me speak of Grian, ye willna feed."

Laughter spurted from her. What might have once been a silvery cascade sounded more like a funeral dirge with bells thrumming in a mournful key.

"Ye doona understand, Fae. I have the upper hand. Ye're helpless. I will feed afore we're done. The question is when."

"Do ye like what ye've become?"

My question broadsided her. She stopped licking my neck. Clearly, she wasn't in the habit of deep thinking, or thinking at all.

My question had come from a place of desperation. No matter how much of the twenty-four hours remained, I was running out of time. My hole wasn't much more than a few centimeters across. I needed triple that to have a prayer of dismantling her grip on me.

Logan and Maeve might come back for me when I wasn't on their heels returning to Faery. Who knew what they'd find.

Because my gaze was glued to the Dearg, I saw the first signs of a descent into madness. Her dark eyes glazed over; her muscles tensed. The fingers grasping my shoulders turned into claws. Growls rose from her throat, low and menacing. The Banshees within my line of vision fell back several paces.

Probably the feral place she usually lived, but my question had kicked the door wide open.

I couldn't withdraw it now.

"Who are you to question me?" she shrieked. "Ye're nothing. My play toy. I'll drain you until nothing is left. And then I'll be Fae, immortal as the rest of you. 'Twon't be but a single day each year I can feed but all of them."

Fuck no, that was not going to happen. Not on my watch.

Stealth was holding me back. No more. I threw every bit of magic at my disposal at the widening breach. I would not go down helpless and paralyzed.

The Dearg's howl said it all. She knew what I was up to. Mouth open, she dove for my throat.

A long drawn-out, "Nooooo," battered my ears. Morgan plowed into the Dearg. Zeke bit through her shoulder amid the crunch of bones. With nothing to hold me back, I blasted through the breach, shattering the creature's hold on me.

Morgan swatted her hard enough to knock her into a nearby wall with the wolf still clinging to her.

Logan was rounding up Banshees, stripping them of power and threatening them with excommunication from the ranks of Faery if they didn't obey him immediately.

Whoever was running them lacked his clout. The women scattered back through whatever portal had spawned them as if the dogs of Hell nipped at their heels.

Morgan was punching the Dearg. Black blood spurted from her nose and ran down her face. Zeke had moved from the shoulder he'd practically torn from her body to a thigh.

"Pah, she tastes wretched," he panted.

I scrambled to my feet. Logan dusted his hands together. "Should hold them for a while."

"You can't really denude them of magic," I pointed out.

"Aye, you know it, and so do I, but they don't."

I chuckled. "Never took you for a poker player. Come on."

We hustled to Morgan, Zeke, and the Dearg. "Can we kill her permanently?" I asked Logan. If anyone was conversant with the lore, it would be him.

He screwed his face into a mass of lines. "Not sure. Maybe if we treat her like any other vampire—"

"Leave me be," the Dearg moaned. "I'll not bother any of you ever again."

Morgan punched her. Adding a broken cheekbone to her broken nose. Zeke yanked hard; a lower leg released, severed at the knee. Black ichor coated the wolf's white fur. He narrowed his eyes to keep the noxious liquid out of them.

An idea came to me. I squatted next to her. Morgan

left off using her as a punching bag. "If we release you. And it's a big if. Ye must give your word ye will quit killing."

"But it's all that keeps me alive," she wailed.

"You are not alive," Morgan snapped. "You're no better than a vampire."

"We can seal you in your coffin," Logan offered, speaking English just like Morgan had. "Sprinkle you with sacred water to ensure you remain dead this time."

"If I doona agree?" Interesting. She'd replied in Gaelic but had clearly understood his tradeoff.

"I'll drive a silver stake through your heart and rid the world of you once and for all," Logan said.

I swallowed surprise. Did he travel with silver stakes because I certainly didn't.

"What's the difference?" Slurred words came from her broken mouth.

"Quite a bit, actually," Logan replied. "If we stake you, you'll turn to naught but bones. If we seal you in your casket, you'll have a chance at eternal rest."

"A chance?"

"Aye. Naught is certain. The gods may deem you irreversibly marked by evil."

"And then what?"

He shrugged. "I don't know."

"She's playing for time." Morgan's fist was still caught in the Dearg's long red hair.

Alarm bells tolled. She'd lost. Was she running out the clock?

On the heels of my question, her form wavered and winked out. Morgan stared at her hand still clutching a hank of hair. Except it was no longer connected with a skull.

"What happened?" she asked.

Logan pounded a fist into his hand. "She outfoxed us."

"But how?" Morgan pushed upright.

Zeke shook himself. The lower leg that had been clutched in his powerful jaws had vanished along with the rest of the Dearg.

"She's only 'alive' one day each year," I explained. "She hit her expiration date."

"Or minute," Morgan said grimly.

I glanced from one to the other. "Maeve took Zoelle to Faery?"

"Aye. We returned for your sorry ass." Logan took a swipe at me.

I jabbed back. "You're enjoying this, mate. Been too long since the Fae went to war—against anyone."

"You two can spar later," Morgan said. "Let's get out of here while we can."

Logan mimed a bow, muttered, "Your wish is my command," and draped a travel spell around us. The damp dungeon walls shimmered and shaded to the black of a journey spell.

"I need a bath," Zeke woofed. *"Not going to tongue-clean this goo off my fur."*

"We'll find you a creek," Morgan promised.

I draped an arm around her. "How come you didn't return with your mother?"

She met my gaze. "Maeve had things well in hand. Simpler for her to only transport one in addition to herself. Plus, I was worried you needed help. And you did."

"I was solving my problem."

"Ha. Didn't look like it. That trashy demon was all over you."

I smothered a snort. "Jealous?"

"Of course not. But I'd have felt guilty forever if anything happened to you while you were helping me."

Color had risen to her cheeks. I drew her closer to me. "Good cover, but you seem jealous."

"Of a demon? Don't be preposterous."

"You two lovebirds can continue this later," Logan said. "We're almost back."

"Whoa. That was quick, even for us," I commented.

"Might have borrowed power from the Banshees to convince them to leave."

Logan had always been a solid tactician. Back when we'd gone to war, he'd ended up platoon leader more often than not.

"Sneaky of you."

He grinned. "It's where I live."

Faery spread around us. I glanced at Morgan standing in blood-splattered clothes. "Let's get you something to wear."

"I want to see Mother."

Zeke woofed, maybe to remind me he wanted to be clean too.

"Come with me." Logan crooked a finger at Zeke. "There's a river where you can freshen up."

"*Where will you be?*" the wolf asked Morgan.

"We have a central clothing depository," I told him. "I will leave her there long enough to find garments that aren't soiled."

"Any idea what time it is on Earth?" she asked.

"Maybe five in the morning," Logan replied.

"Good. I have time."

"For what?" Logan arched fair brows.

"To get to work at seven. I can change, check on Mother, and hurry back to the lodging house."

"Pfft." Logan flapped a hand our way. "What is it with you and working in the mortal world. Your energies are far better spent here."

"His, maybe," Morgan retorted. "I'm not Fae."

"Today, you acted like one of us," Logan told her. "You were courageous and resourceful. You could have returned with your mother, yet you chose to remain in the thick of things."

"Thank you, but Fae don't corner the market on courage." Morgan stood tall. I was proud of her.

"And you accused me of being pigheaded," he muttered before stalking off with Zeke trotting behind him.

"You could have just said thank you and stopped there," I observed.

She grinned. "Yeah, but it wouldn't have been me. Now, where are those clothes? And do you have some sort of speed magic wash for what's on my body?"

I held out a hand. She laced her fingers with mine. "Goddess forbid you be anyone other than you."

She started to laugh. I joined in as we wended deeper into Faery. Having her by my side felt right in a way very little else has, but she had a grand role to play. One I couldn't reveal to her. Maybe Zoelle would come around enough to disclose whatever she knew. Or perhaps she'd choose to remain silent. Simpler for me if she recognized what her silence had cost and rectified the problem.

Still, I wasn't her. Neither was I privy to her thought patterns.

The queen of witches—once Morgan picked up the banner and came into her own—didn't require a consort. Given their history of eschewing men entirely, I wouldn't have even a peripheral role to play.

"You're quiet."

I slapped wards around my thoughts. Not telling her was one thing; having her pluck the truth from my mind in an unguarded moment quite another.

"Been a long night," I said and guided her through an

open door into an enormous room. "Women's clothing runs along that wall." I pointed at a series of cupboards, armoires, and shelves. "We have every style from about the 1300s on, so you'll want to start at the extreme right end where the modern garments are."

"Thank you. Is there a way to flash clean what's on me?"

"Of course. Follow me."

CHAPTER FIFTEEN, MORGAN

Damien left after he showed me the conveyor belt to place my soiled clothing on. Much like one we'd had at the Coven guild house, it passed items beneath a laser that removed soil, stains, and sweat. While it was working, I rummaged through bins and closets, selecting serviceable trousers and tops. Since no one seemed to be using any of it—and there was a lot—I chose a couple of outfits beyond what was on my body.

My final stop before collecting the clothing I'd worn in here was at a sink perched in a corner. I washed blood off my hands and face, and called it even. If I'd found the sink before I'd dressed, I might have been more thorough.

As it was, I wanted to find Mother, assure myself she was on the mend, and return in time to pick up my early morning kitchen shift.

Damien met me in the hall with a fluffy white Zeke by his side. The wolf wasn't fond of baths, but he hated stinky crud in his fur even worse.

"Do you mind?" I held up the stack of borrowed items.

"Not at all. It solves one problem. You'd said you needed clothing."

We retraced our steps. Maybe we did. Faery was huge and mazelike. For all I knew, the vast warren of corridors shifted at the whim of the land.

"How's Mother?"

"Still unconscious."

I frowned. "Um, that's not good, is it?"

"She's been through a lot. Give her a chance."

"Is Sita with her?"

Damien smiled softly. "Hasn't left her side."

If anyone could pull her through, it would be her familiar.

"What have the healers said?" I pressed for details.

Damien shook his head. "I've been with Logan and the council preparing for backlash from today."

"Why? Banshees are actually Fae, and we sort of rid the world of a pernicious demon. Or kicked that can down the road for another year. Who could fault us for either?"

He stopped walking and spun me to look at him. "You know damn good and well. Your Coven—or the part of it involved in kidnapping and torturing your mother—will cite interference. Such is strictly forbidden in every mage's covenant."

"But how could we have known they were involved?" I asked in saccharine tones. "I saw Banshees and a Dearg. No witches in sight other than yours truly."

He choked out a snort. "Why you minx, you."

I kicked my shoulders back. "I'm nothing of the kind. We heard rumors of trouble at the castle near my old guild house. My brand-new Fae friends were kind enough to come with me, exploring."

I paused to suck in a breath. "Nothing we found had the Coven's mark stenciled in stone beyond a few ancient beacons. Sure, we found Mother, but she wasn't able to tell us how she got there. Because she was in distress, we hustled her back to Faery for healing."

He angled his head to one side. "Why wouldn't we have left her at the Coven guild house?"

I grinned. "Do you know where it is?"

I'd seen it in Maeve's vision but had no idea where to find it. "Good point. So we moved her to Faery as a stopgap while we worked to locate her kinswomen."

I nodded. "Exactly. Of course, I argued against involving the Coven since they rejected me."

"But the Fae council overruled you." Damien finished my thought.

"Something like that. It gets you out from under the worst of potential fallout."

"If not an outright war," Damien muttered. "'Tis what the council fears."

"You'd win," I said flatly. Alongside the words, I wanted the Coven to suffer.

"What happens when the Coven demands we hand Zoelle over to them?"

"She's too fragile to be moved."

"They'll say they have their own healers," Damien argued.

We started walking again, this time faster. "You're overthinking this," I told him. "If the Coven—or some of them—made a deal with the devil, they won't want the rest of the sisterhood to find out about it. They'll play their cards close to the vest."

An unpleasant thought swatted me. "They know exactly what they did to her," I murmured. "A self-perpetuating spell could keep her laid up permanently."

"Our healers would find it."

"Maybe. Our magic is different." The more I talked, the more worried I became.

We'd reached a nexus where corridors spread out from the one we'd traveled like spokes on a wagon wheel. Damien hesitated, spreading power ahead of us.

"You're not certain of the way?"

"Not entirely," he admitted.

I should have kept my mouth shut, but it's never been my strong suit. "Why not?"

"Faery is rarely the same two visits running."

Aha. There it was. I'd suspected as much.

"This way." Hooking a hand around my arm, he directed us into the second walkway from the right.

I sought Mother with enchantment of my own. To my surprise, she was close. Sure enough, the corridor widened. We passed diaphanous veils and entered a large circular room. The only occupied bed was Mother's.

I hesitated, taking her in from a few feet away. One Fae sat next to her weaving runes with her fingertips. They twirled around Mother in a circle before being absorbed as new ones took their place. Another Fae stood behind the bed chanting softly.

Both women wore long, white robes sashed in blue. One had violet hair; the other's was black. Sharp facial planes and pointed ears lent an ethereal aspect.

They'd cleaned Mother up, brushed her tangled hair. It fanned out across the pillow like living flames. By contrast, her face was pale, freckles standing out across her nose and cheeks. The gentle rise and fall of her chest didn't seem forced.

Sita squawked and flew to me, lighting on a shoulder. *"Thank you for finding her."*

"Thank you for standing vigil."

The hawk bobbed her head. *"I will remain, no matter what."*

What she meant was even if Mother rejected resurrecting their bond, the hawk wouldn't desert her.

Zeke padded across the room and nudged Mother's

hand with his nose. Her lips curved into a half smile. Was she more aware of her surroundings than we believed?

I joined the wolf and bowed to the two healers. "Thank you for caring for Mother. How is she?"

Two sets of silver eyes raked me up one side and down the other. I stood still beneath their scrutiny.

The one with fluffy violet hair frowned. "But you're not, erm, related. Not directly."

Defensiveness settled around me, a shield against hurtful words. "You're mistaken. She is my mother. She's been with me my entire life."

The dark-haired one came around the bed and pressed a palm over my forehead. Another shot of magic coursed through me. "This witch may have raised you," the Fae said, "yet you do not share blood."

My mouth flapped open and shut. Screaming she was wrong wouldn't buy me shit. I sucked in a steadying breath, blew it out, and did it again. I could sort genetics later.

"How is she?" I asked the healers for a second time.

"She should be awake," the dark-haired one said.

"Yet she is not," the other chimed in.

"Did you look for indwelling spells?" I asked.

Both women sent pointed glances skittering my way. "Of course," the violet-haired one replied.

"We found two of them," the other Fae explained.

"Which we removed," the first Fae said.

Mother moaned, tossing this way and that.

Both Fae took up their previous positions with runes and chanting.

"Best if you leave for now," one murmured.

"Aye, your presence upsets her," the other added.

But I'm her daughter. Or am I?

What secrets had Mother sat on all these years?

Sita winged back to Mother's headboard. Zeke licked her hand and trotted to me.

"I'll return in a few hours," I said.

"We'll be here," the dark-haired Fae replied.

Grateful Mother was in a place the Coven couldn't penetrate, I followed Damien out of the infirmary.

"She doesn't want to waken," Zeke said.

"Why would you say that?" Damien asked him.

"Because she knew I was there and chose to remain asleep. Sita thinks the same."

"Shall I take us to my room or yours?" Damien asked.

"Doesn't matter." I still clutched the stack of garments close.

"Then we'll start in your room."

The muted light of Faery shaded first to black and then to the familiar off-white walls of my chamber. Daylight was just breaking, turning the sky pale pink. I tugged a drawer open and placed my new-to-me garments in it.

Zeke put his paws on the windowsill, looking outside.

"Are you all right?" Damien asked.

"Not even close."

He was giving me space, not trying to touch or crowd me. I wanted to throw myself into his arms, feel the living solidness of him stretched against me.

Pride won the day.

"What's the worst part?" he asked softly.

Worst wore a lot of faces. "Probably that she's not really my mother. If it's true, and your healers have no reason to lie, where'd I come from? It's bad enough not being aware who my father was, but Zoelle must know the truth. About everything.

And she'd never told me.

Damien closed the distance between us and folded his big arms around me. The scents of a restless ocean and damp evergreens wafted around me. He stroked my hair.

"We'll figure this out."

"I have to, but you don't." My voice was muffled in the folds of his woolen jacket.

"Stop being so insufferably brave."

I wriggled, trying to get loose, but he didn't let go.

Zeke gave a little yip. He still stood on his hind legs staring out the window.

"What is it?" I asked.

"Witches. Two of them."

Damien released me and strode to the window. He vanished from sight but was still in the room, so he must have warded himself.

"Crap. Didn't take them long," he muttered.

Curiosity drove me to the window. Sure enough, Lilith

and Mirabelle stood on the sidewalk next to steps leading into the lodging house. They'd already seen Zeke, so I didn't bother cloaking myself. Waste of magic. They already knew exactly where I was.

They'd probably known from the moment I trudged up the front steps in search of a roof over my head.

Anger turned my tired muscles to bricks. "Fuck this. I'm going down there."

"The hell you are." Invisible hands gripped my upper arms.

"They kicked me out. They do not get to spy on me."

The curtain moved across the window, blocking us from view. Zeke jumped down. Damien shimmered back into view. He still had a firm hold on me.

"Keep your eye on the prize," he hissed. "They're trying to rattle you because they're furious about losing Zoelle."

"Why do they hate me? What did I do to deserve any of this?" My voice shrilled. Tears were ridiculously close to the surface. I never cried, yet my eyes burned.

"Pull yourself together." His tone was gruff. It slapped sense into me. The tears retreated.

In their place rose a vow. I'd get even no matter how long it took. For now, though, we had bigger problems. "They're probably planting hex bags," I said. "To make everyone who lives here miserable. I should leave."

"I'll find the bags," he said. "Before I go to work."

"They'll just plant more." My voice was so dry and dull, I scarcely recognized it.

"We'll dismantle them too. Eventually, they'll get tired."

"Ha. You don't know them. They want Mother back, and they'll make my life hell until we turn her over."

He shook me, not hard, but it got my attention. "We will never do that."

There it was again, *we*. "Why are you helping me? I don't understand."

He kissed my forehead. Heat shot all the way to my toes.

"Because I like you. Our paths crossed for a reason. If we're patient, the future will become clear."

"Can't we ask Maeve? Sometimes Lilith would clarify events."

He shook his head. "Maeve doesn't operate that way. If she knows something, she keeps it to herself so as to not influence the future."

"I see."

"You need to get moving. I'll collect the hex bags—or whatever mayhem they strewed. Once I have them, I'll drop them in Faery to be stripped of their power. And then I'm off to work. See you tonight. We'll check on Zoelle again after supper."

Before I could protest about him planning my life for me, he was gone. I pushed the drawer with my clothes in it shut, ran the hairbrush through my unruly locks, and headed for the kitchen with Zeke next to me.

We were right on time. Hard to believe considering how jam-packed the last few hours had been. The cook smiled and put me to work peeling potatoes. He'd put out a dish of scraps for Zeke and a bowl of water. The wolf—ensconced in his doggie glamour—made short work of the food and lapped noisily.

I wanted to know what was in the hex bags. What manner of fuckery had the Coven planned for the innocents who lived in this building? I was holding the knife so hard, my knuckles turned white. Once Damien left the bags in Faery, I'd never find out. He could describe them, but he wouldn't recognize the significance of their contents. Maeve might, but no guarantee she'd lay eyes on them.

Calming myself rose to the fore. Getting mad wouldn't buy me crap. Neither would taking off to catch up with Damien. Hell, I probably couldn't get into Faery on my own.

"Everything all right?" the cook asked.

"Yeah, fine. Didn't sleep very well."

"Tonight will be better." His words held kindness, and they smote me. Why was everyone being nice to me? Even when I'd lived in the guild house, the sisterhood was more bitchy than kind.

"I sure hope so."

Soft snores rose from Zeke's open mouth. He lay on his side with his back against the far wall.

I should catch a nap after breakfast. Instead, I'd do a bit of sleuthing. A visit to the guild house was in order. Two could play the "how many ways can I fuck you over?" game.

If they thought they were going to steamroll over me, I had a few surprises in store for them. We carried the same magic, and mine has always been strong. Before I was done, they'd be crying for mercy. Quite aside from their shenanigans today, they should suffer for what they'd put Mother through.

Yeah, the mother who wasn't one. Or not mine, apparently.

With visions of revenge fueling me, I moved from food preparation to laying out plates and silverware. We'd see who had the last word. I wasn't going down without a fight. Hell, if I had my way, I wasn't going down at all.

CHAPTER SIXTEEN, DAMIEN

Morgan hadn't been kidding about hex bags. I didn't actually expect to find any. I'd only looked to humor her. By the time I was done, ten of the nasty things were tucked in a pocket with spells laid around them to protect me from their evil.

I didn't bother dissecting them, just dumped them into the trash container designed to defuse spells gone awry. Even with it all, I was more or less on time at the jobsite. I beat the foreman in and hoped to hell he'd gotten off his overtime bandwagon.

As I hefted boards and my nail gun, I lost myself in the joy of simple tasks. Ones that had beginnings and ends. It was why I was loathe to quit. I enjoyed building things, real things without a scrap of enchantment.

Those days were rapidly drawing to a close, though.

Wandering along scaffoldings and slinging a hammer were an indulgence. Faery needed me. Morgan too, although she'd rather die than admit it.

The healers' statements about her mother not being related by blood weren't exactly a surprise. Not after the revelations from Lilith and her kinswomen. Among other things, it meant Zoelle knew a lot.

Probably everything.

Whether she'd choose to share her knowledge remained to be seen. My vote was for no. She'd held out all the years of Morgan's life. Granted, a few key elements had shifted. No one passes through kidnap and torture unscathed. And being separated from her familiar.

If we hadn't rescued her, the Coven would never have let her go.

My thoughts were growing circular. The Coven was out for blood. It explained their presence outside the boardinghouse early this morning. I should have told Morgan to be careful, except she didn't need to hear the words from my lips to know how unscrupulous her fellow witches were.

Someone yelled at me to move on to drywall. I rappelled to the ground to fix the heavy sheets to a dolly so we could position them where they were needed.

Morgan was in an untenable position. I haven't always been overly fond of the Fae, and some of the council's decisions have been plain shortsighted. Still, my kin have never targeted me, never told me to leave permanently.

For the first time, I put myself in Morgan's spot. Truly placed myself there. My heart broke for her. She'd had everything in her life yanked out from under her with no explanation.

I debated telling her what I'd seen in Maeve's display, but I trusted our seer. She'd been exceedingly clear to keep my mouth shut. Never mind, my silence was linked to a blood bond. If I broke it, there'd be unpleasant consequences.

Even if I ran that gauntlet and told Morgan, what would she do with the information?

The various Covens didn't have any connection, one with the other. She couldn't darken the door of her erstwhile one. Seemed unlikely she'd knock on the door of the next nearest Coven and introduce herself as their queen.

My jaw was tight. I loosened it before I cracked a tooth.

I could see it now. Whoever answered the door would slam it in her face the moment she stated her business. "Hi, I'm Morgan. You don't know it yet, but I'm destined to rule you. All of you."

"Hey, dude. Look sharp," someone yelled.

I ducked in time to avoid the edge of a sheet of drywall dangling from a crane and called out, "Sorry."

"Where's your hard hat?" the foreman shouted.

Oops. I retrieved it from atop one of my toolboxes and settled it into place.

The rest of the day passed without incident. I made myself scarce before the foreman hit me up for more overtime. Maybe he'd found someone else hungry for the double wages.

I hoped so.

Back at the boardinghouse, I cleaned up and headed for the dining room expecting to see Morgan and Zeke.

They weren't there.

At first, I assumed they were in the kitchen, but a hasty shot of seeking magic told me otherwise. My appetite fled. Where in the hell were they? Had the cook sent her on another errand? Shopping, perhaps?

I didn't want to ask him directly, so I made a quick trip through his mind. Something odd about the feel of him jabbed me, but I didn't have time to sort it out.

He was as worried as I was. She hadn't shown up for either lunch or dinner preparation. He'd considered reporting her missing but hadn't since he didn't know her last name.

Besides, no one in law enforcement worried themselves about vagrants who were one step up from homeless. Far as they were concerned, Morgan was another female who'd hit the skids. Maybe her pimp found her and had forced her back into service.

I ducked out of the food line and laid my plate on top of the stack. Layering "don't look here" spells, I faded out of the dining hall. Hopefully, no one would remember I'd even been here.

My first stop was Morgan's room. Her energy ran strong here, and I had no trouble setting a tracking spell in motion. She'd traveled on foot; so did I. When I'm invisible, I can travel fast. Not too many places she could have gone. She'd be worried about Zoelle, but she couldn't enter Faery without me or another of the Fae present.

Not easily.

When my track led to a rambling old Victorian on Queen Anne Hill, I recognized it from the vision in Maeve's display.

The Coven guild house.

Fuck it! I slammed a fist into a nearby tree, wincing when my knuckles scraped against rough bark.

Why had she come here by herself?

Even with me, it would have been little better than a fool's errand.

These witches had it in for her.

I lingered on the corner that separated the magical world of the Coven from the normal one. Mortals could certainly see the mansion, but they'd be rebuffed if they knocked at any of its many gateways.

Witch enchantment wouldn't have an effect on me,

but me showing up at a door would be stupid. For one thing, it would make the witches aware of my connection with Morgan. They already knew she'd aligned herself with some of the Fae. No reason to give them further ammunition. Of course, they might have identified me in the meadow where Sita had intercepted us.

Hard to know about these things.

I balanced from foot to foot. I could tighten my warding and teleport inside.

A risky move. Surely, they'd have sentinels set, beacons that would react to my magic and give away my presence.

How could I help her?

Damn it. I wished I'd studied more about Coven structure the night I'd crammed research into my mind.

Not going to help me now.

Should I teleport to Faery for reinforcements?

Eh, also not the best idea unless I wanted to fan the flames of a brand new turf war.

No one likes being hamstrung, and, no matter which path I selected, there'd be big downsides. Fallout's never stopped me before, but I refused to be the lynchpin spawning a war between witches and Fae.

We'd win, but not without cost.

Admitting I was stuck was tough. I couldn't move forward. All I could do was retreat. It rankled.

I started to retrace my steps, but five minutes later I hadn't stirred. What was I waiting for? A sign from Danu?

The moon chose that moment to slither from under heavy cloud cover, casting the darkened street in a silvery glow. I glanced skyward. Serendipity? Was Artemis standing in for Danu and telling me something?

If so, what?

The Celts had a rather large hand in forming light and dark Fae, Sidhe too. But they'd been absent from Earth for hundreds of years. Was the moonbeam encouragement?

I opened my magical center and waited. It wasn't wise to remain like this for long, not in proximity to a Coven guild house. If they posted sentries, they'd sense me no matter how thick my ward.

A minute ticked by. Then two then three.

Nothing.

I resurrected my shielding and drew the heart of my enchantment close once again.

Talk about a waste of time.

A doddering old woman would be more on point than me.

Since I was getting nowhere fast, I forced an about face. I'd melt into a nearby alleyway and teleport to Faery where I could kick this latest development around with Logan and Maeve and a few others.

They'd tell me to leave well enough alone, or I thought they would.

I hadn't gotten ten paces from my corner vantage point when Morgan's unique energy buffeted me. She and

Zeke fell into step. "What are you doing here?" she panted.

The wolf licked my hand, tail pluming.

I twirled and faced them. She wasn't warded and looked much the worse for wear. Her clothing was soaked; odd since it wasn't raining.

A quick glance about told me we were alone. I dropped my warding. "How'd you see through my protections?" I demanded. "Furthermore, what the fuck were you doing here? You missed lunch and dinner."

Her chest rose and fell as she worked to catch her breath. "Yeah. I know. Couldn't be helped. I got in easy as pie, but then I couldn't get out."

I dragged her into the same alley I'd planned to teleport from. "You're talking in riddles, woman."

"Suppose I am." She laid a hand over her upper chest and took a few deep breaths. "They changed things since I left. Marker beacons are everywhere. I got lucky getting inside. Missed them all, but they move on their own. One landed almost on top of us. I didn't dare move; I'd have set it off."

Zeke woofed softly.

"Waited it out," she went on. "The beacon had to move again sooner or later. And it did about a minute ago. I broke clear as soon as opportunity presented itself. Wasn't sure how long the window would last."

I wanted to shake her. "What you did was stupid. Why didn't you wait for me?"

The wolf stopped licking my hand and growled. Rebuking his bondmate was out of bounds.

"What could you have done?" Her tone sharpened. "Your magic sticks out like a wolf in a sheep herd. They'd have apprehended us for sure."

"I'd have kept you safe." My voice was gruff. I did not want to betray how frantic I'd been about her safety.

"Yeah, well, I managed okay on my own." She poked my chest with her index finger. "I'm still a witch, one of them. I know how they think. You don't."

Worry never brings out the best in me. "Apparently, you didn't anticipate the addition of magical sentries."

She screwed her mouth into a moue. "That was low. Did you come all this way to criticize me? If so, you can teleport the fuck out of here." A shudder wracked her body.

I parked my ego at the door. Maybe she was right about me being more of a hindrance than a help inside the guild house. Given the choice, I hadn't entered on my own. Rather than my hurt feelings, I focused on Morgan. She must be freezing in her wet garments.

I touched her shoulder. "Sorry. I apologize. How'd you get wet?"

"Did it on purpose so they'd have a harder time apprehending me. Water doesn't exactly mute our magic, but it diffuses it, makes it tougher to pinpoint. Can we go back now? I owe the cook an explanation."

By way of an answer, I draped a spell over her and

instructed it to take us to her room. Zeke took up his position, paws on the sill, staring out into the dark as he kept the watch. I turned around while Morgan dressed, offering the illusion of privacy.

"You were there for a while," I ventured. "Did you learn anything?"

"You can turn around now."

I did. She'd slithered into dry pants and a blue woolen top. Breath swooshed from her.

I gave it another couple of seconds before I sat on the edge of the sewing table. Morgan was gathering her long tresses into a queue and fastening the thick strands low on the nape of her neck.

"To answer your question," she said, "I didn't learn anything I didn't already know. They're all spun out about losing Mother. My best guess is she knows something, and they do not want her telling me or anyone else."

I'd already figured that part out, but then I had inside information. "Whatever it is"—I felt my way cautiously—"at least some of them are also aware. It can't only be your mother."

"It could be mostly Mother. The others tortured her for a reason. If they knew everything she did, there'd have been no reason."

"Good point."

Morgan shook her head. "How could I have been so dense? Fuck. I lived there for years and years. It never occurred to me my sisters were holding secrets about me —ones they'd go to great odds to conceal."

She closed her teeth over her lower lip until I saw pinpricks of blood pool. "What could it possibly be? What's wrong with me that they had to take Draconian measures to separate us?"

I poured extra layers around my mind so she wouldn't pluck the truth from me. "Your mother is your best bet to answer that."

"We need to pay Faery a visit, but first I should make my apologies to the cook."

"Probably best if you wait until morning," I pointed out. "You're not going to endear yourself by waking him up."

Her eyes widened. "What time is it?"

"Closing on eleven."

"Yeah. Time flies and all that crap."

Zeke growled low. I hustled to the window and sent seeking magic zinging into the darkness.

Morgan glided between the wolf and me. "Are they back?"

No need to spell out who "they" were.

"'Fraid so," I muttered. "Do you suppose they came for their hex bags?"

"No. Once they're in place, they stay there." She paused to suck in a breath. "But they'll figure out soon enough they're gone."

"And?" I struggled to make a connection between missing hex bags and what they'd do next.

Morgan stepped away from the window and gestured for me to do the same. She snapped her fingers at Zeke, but he didn't move.

"You picked up the bags," she reminded me. "Means your magic is scattered all over where they were. Whoever's out there—and I didn't bother to home in on their identities—will know a Fae interfered."

"It gets worse. The hex bags are in one of our magical lockers in Faery to defuse their evil."

Meddling with other types of magic is strictly forbidden. We'd done nothing but lately, from rescuing Zoelle to spying on the Coven to my casual treatment of the hex bags. I'd been focused on protecting passersby, not on hiding my magic.

Shortsighted of me.

"Naught I can do about it now," I muttered. "Never occurred to me they weren't done with those bags. Before you, I've never seen any witch outside her Coven."

Furrows formed between Morgan's brows. "The times are changing, and not in ways that I like. Tell you what. I'm going to leave a note for the cook. Apologize and alert him I'll be in the kitchen bright and early, and—"

"Except you might not be," I cut in. "Depending on how things play out in Faery, you could be held up."

"But I have hours," she protested.

"Up to you," I told her. "I need to stop by my room and grab a jacket. Meet you by the front door."

Her brows formed twin question marks. "What do you have in mind?"

"Better if you don't know." I scratched Zeke's ears and left the room, taking care to tread lightly so as not to waken anyone.

I selected two crystals from the collection I kept in my quarters and infused them with destructive magic. Next, I crafted illusion around them to make them look and feel like hex bags. When the witches picked them up, believing they were the same ones they'd left, the crystals would begin a slow, insidious poisoning.

I couldn't kill them, but I could warp their minds, so they'd no longer be capable of manipulating magic. After a quickie test run with a plain crystal, I directed the other two to plonk down not too far from where two witches patrolled.

Excellent. This could be managed from a distance.

"Not the front door, after all," I sent Morgan's way. *"Meet me in my room."*

As I waited for her and Zeke, I plotted out the next few hours. We'd go to Faery, ensure the hex bags were destroyed—in case anyone came looking for them—and see if Zoelle was conscious.

If she was, we'd start with questions. On the other hand, if she was still comatose, I wasn't above using magic to bring her around. The healers would protest loudly, but Morgan needed answers.

Better for them to come from Zoelle than from me. Besides, all I possessed was a snapshot. There had to be more to the story than my brief glimpse of the witches arguing.

After a light tap, the lock turned. Morgan and Zeke slipped in and pushed the door shut.

"What'd you do?" she asked. "The witches left."

"Baited a trap. You'd be surprised what can be spelled to look like a hex bag. I'm sick of them spying on us. If we send back a couple of problems, maybe they'll quit."

She smiled with lots of teeth. "You're full of surprises."

"Oh, am I now?"

She mock slugged me. "Let's get moving. I really would like to be back in time for breakfast preparations."

I mimed a bow and draped a journey casting over us all.

"Next stop, Faery." My tone was jaunty.

"Is there a way for me to go there on my own?"

The question took me aback. I could see why she'd want to, though. It meant safety from the Coven. And Zoelle was there.

"Not sure. But I'll ask and see if we can't get that set up for you."

"Thanks." She slipped a hand beneath my arm. "I still

don't know why you're being so nice to me, but I appreciate it."

Because I'm falling in love with you.

Whoa. Better not let that cat out of the bag.

"Damien?"

I patted her hand. "Nothing. You need a friend. I was in the right place at the right time. Glad to be able to help."

She leaned into me. "There's more to this. When I get breathing space, I'll figure it out."

The press of her body against my side was alluring, but I couldn't let myself think about it. Faery bloomed around us, welcoming me home.

"Let's drop you off with the healers," I said. "And then I'll take care of the hex bags."

"Thank you."

Zeke woofed, tail pluming.

I guided us down several corridors before locating the one leading to the infirmary. "No thanks needed. The healers are expecting you. I already told them we were headed their way."

I wanted to kiss her. Instead, I did an about face and set off at a lope for the subterranean cavern where I'd stashed the bags. Hopefully, Zoelle was awake and, by the time I showed up, Morgan would be well on her way to filling in the many gaps in her history.

I was midway through destroying the bags for good when shrieks echoed through my head. Morgan was shouting my name in telepathy so raw and tortured, all of Faery would probably come at a dead run. Dropping what I was doing, I sprinted for the infirmary.

Had the Coven found a way in?

No reason to torment myself; I'd find out soon enough.

CHAPTER SEVENTEEN, MORGAN

The corridor seemed longer than it had the last time I'd trod its length. Try as I might, I couldn't feel Mother's energy. Had the healers covered her in concealment spells?

Zeke whined but didn't voice his concerns.

One of the white-clad Fae met us where the passageway opened into the round room I remembered. Mother was still their only patient. She lay on a pallet near the far wall with runes hovering over her in the still air. Unlike human hospitals, this one smelled of wildflowers and the ocean, not antiseptic.

"How is she?" I asked, keeping my voice quiet.

"We are worried," the healer replied.

"Aye," another chimed in. "She should have wakened by now. Naught we do has made any difference. She's deeper in trance than when she arrived."

Sita squawked from her position near Mother's head and stroked her beak through her long, red hair. Zeke trotted to the hawk, offering moral support.

I crossed the room and knelt near the head of Mother's pallet. Taking one of her thin hands in mine, I stroked it and murmured endearments. Could she hear me?

No way to tell. Her eyes moved beneath translucent lids as if she were dreaming. The healers had come close, chanting in Gaelic. Runes switched direction, whirling the other way and changing color from violet to blues and greens.

Mother moaned softly. Her fingers twitched in the hand I held.

"You must try," I told her. "Reach for the light, Mother. Don't let them rob you of everything."

I sent tendrils into her mind but ran into a blank wall.

"Did you block access to her?" I asked the Fae and sucked in an anxious breath.

They shook their heads.

"Nay. She's been thus since she arrived. We can't break through, either," one murmured.

"And if we can't, the runes will be stymied too," the other said.

I didn't ask what purpose they served. Since they weren't working, it didn't matter.

Lying next to Mother, I gathered her into my arms

shocked by how she'd devolved into not much more than skin stretched over bones.

"Mother. Please. I need you. Come back from where you wander."

Zeke licked her face and arms. Sita quorked mournfully. It sounded like a funeral dirge, and I started to tell her to lay off, but she loved Mother too.

We remained like that for a while, a tableau frozen in time, each of us urging Mother to fight whatever kept her apart from us. Finally, one arm wrapped loosely around me.

"Morgan?" she rasped in a voice that sounded as if she hadn't used it in centuries.

"Yes, it's me. Zeke is here too. And Sita."

The bird squawked.

Mother struggled, so I let go of her. "You shouldn't have come," she said. "Not to our compound in the Old Country and not here, either. It's a trap. One they set to snare you too."

"You're not thinking straight," I began.

Shrieks erupted from her. She grasped her head as if it hurt.

"Move aside." The Fae healer was brusque as she pushed me out of the way and laid her hands on Mother's arms. The other Fae held her legs.

Mother cursed and squealed and screamed. Flesh sloughed off her in bloody hanks.

What the fuck? Who was doing this to her.

Far from an alarmist, I cried for Damien. Maybe he could fix this.

The room filled with Fae, but all my attention was on Mother. Her body was disintegrating before my eyes. Stabs of pain racked me. At first, I pegged it as emotional. Watching Mother suffer was agonizing.

But then I identified a definite drag with the Coven's stamp all over it. Mother had known and tried to warn me. I built wards, but was I quick enough? Darts riddled with witchy enchantment pricked as they sought entry.

Damien skidded to my side and dragged me upright.

A different sort of enchantment scoured me, doing battle with witch power.

"How in the hell did they get in here?" he shouted.

"They didn't, not exactly," Logan answered.

"Explain that, then." Damien pointed at the bloody pulp surrounding the woman who'd once been my mother.

"Can't."

"Do something," I shrilled and jerked out of Damien's grip. Crying and panting, I threw myself to my knees and patted Mother's body parts back into place, doing my damnedest to bind them with magic so they'd stick.

Her clear green eyes flew open, all traces of madness long gone. "Let me go," she said in a voice that sounded like her. "Let me go. They'll never leave off."

"Why?" I moaned. "Why? Is it because of me?"

"Aye and nay." The bloody bits I'd cobbled back

together exploded showering me and everyone close with gore. Heedless of the mess, I held her tight, but what was left of her dissolved into a red mist.

Sita's desolate cries accelerated. She pushed her body between me and Mother, pain sheeting from her beak as she mourned her mistress.

Hands gripped my shoulders and pulled me upright. "She's gone," Damien said. "Nothing more you can do for her."

Tears flooded my eyes; inchoate sounds burst from me. Witches are immortal. How could Mother be gone?

Damien held me against him.

The healers scurried this way and that, but I couldn't see them. "What are they doing with her?" I demanded.

"Making certain the Coven doesn't get hold of her essence." Damien's tone was grim.

I kicked my head back and stared at him. "So they're here?" And then I remembered how they'd made a play for me too.

"Like Logan said. Aye and nay. They found a way to breach our borders with enough energy to zero in on Zoelle. It worked because she was one of them."

Furrows formed between his brows; green eyes bored into me. "Did you feel them?"

I nodded. "Either they didn't try very hard or my warding stymied them."

Zeke padded next to us. *"You're stronger than they are,"* he woofed.

Sita swooped near and lit on his withers, still cawing sadly. *"I hate them,"* she quorked. *"Hate them. I will gather every avian familiar. We will make them pay for what they did to my beloved."*

"You'd have to return to the Coven," Damien told her. "Do you really want to take that chance?"

Sita hung her head; her beak clacked a few times. *"But I must avenge her. If not me, then who?"*

"There's me, her daughter," I reminded the hawk.

Her sort of daughter, an inner voice reminded me. Now I'd never find out the truth. About anything. No one else would tell me. Hell no. They'd banished me.

"We are done," one of the healers trilled.

"Aye, you can sit with your mother without fear of assimilation from her enemies," the other added.

Tears still pelted down my cheeks. My eyes were gritty and hot. Damien let go of me, and I sank to Mother's side. The healers had put her body back together, but life no longer flowed within its confines.

I stroked her sunken cheeks, her translucent fingers. Whether we shared blood or not, she was my oldest and best friend. My only one in the entire Coven.

"This was all my fault," I choked out. "She told me not to abandon my glamour, but I did anyway. It's what started everything."

"They took her away before you did that," Damien reminded me.

So they had, but I'd assumed she was off on some kind

of mission or vacation. It never occurred to me the sisters had shanghaied her.

So much I didn't know.

I sat next to Mother's body for a long time with Zeke and Sita. Damien, Logan, and others conversed quietly.

A hand dropped onto my shoulder. When I looked around, one of the healers nodded at me. "It is time," she said.

"For what?" At least I'd run out of tears, but a horrible, hollow, empty feeling dogged me.

"We must commit Zoelle's body to the flames to ensure the sanctity of her eternal soul."

I blinked stupidly. "You're going to burn Mother?"

"It's the only way," Damien's deep voice concurred.

The Coven lacked death rituals. That the Fae had any surprised me since they're immortal too. I rose slowly and prayed to Hecate as the healers loaded Mother onto a wheeled bier.

We fell into step behind it as the healers wound lower and lower into Faery. Finally, we came to the shores of a lake with black water. The bier changed form and became a slender canoe that slid into the waves. When it was about fifty feet from shore, it burst into flames.

Zeke howled. Sita shrilled a tuneless dirge as misery poured from her.

I watched the burning craft float farther and farther away.

"Do not mourn me, Daughter. I am free now," brushed

my mind just before Mother and the craft vanished from sight.

We retraced our steps. Damien's arm lay heavy around my shoulders in silent support.

"What do you want to do?" he asked.

My mind was a jumble. "Huh? Want to do when?"

"Right now. If we leave, you'll be back in time for breakfast preparations on Earth. Or you could leave that life and—"

"And what?" Bitterness lined my question. Everything that had ever meant anything—except Zeke—had been stripped from me. "My entire life has been a sham."

"Do you want to find out why you feel that way?"

Something about his wording snagged my attention. "Maybe, but not right now. I need normal and mindless."

He stroked hair back from my cheek, tucking it behind one ear. "Then it's back to the boardinghouse."

"How is that normal?" I mumbled. "I've only spent a handful of days there."

"Morgan." He dropped both hands onto my shoulders. "You've hit a rough patch. Throwing a pity party won't help."

I twisted from under his grip. "Who are you to tell me how to feel or what to do?"

"Your friend."

Shame swamped me. "Sorry. I'm sorry." The tears I'd been certain I ran out of flooded my eyes.

"It's okay. You needn't apologize to me. Come on. Let's go back."

"*Where will I go?*" Sita squawked. "*I have no one.*"

"Would you like to remain in Faery?" Damien asked the hawk.

She spread her wings. "*Could I? Just for a little while.*"

"Stay as long as you'd like," he told her. "Logan and I already discussed it."

The hawk brushed her beak across his cheek before flying away.

Damien swathed Zeke and me in a journey spell; we traded Faery for his room. Dawn was breaking.

"I'll see you at dinner," Damien said.

"What are you doing today?" I asked, but then held up a hand. "Never mind. Not my affair."

"Glad you asked. I'm going to work." Something unreadable played across his sharply defined features. In that moment, he looked far more Fae than human.

"What aren't you saying?" I blurted.

"Our time here is drawing to a close. The boardinghouse has served me well." A smile curved his lips. "I didn't understand why I picked this place, but it was the venue that brought us together."

"Are you expecting we'll remain together?" The moment the words were out, my face grew hot. I so did not need romantic anything, but something about him sang to my soul, had from the first moment I'd laid eyes on him standing at the bottom of the stairs.

Was I only now admitting it to myself?

"Hard to say what the goddess has in store. Best get going so you're not late for breakfast prep."

Mother's words about being free rattled around my mind as I checked the corridor and snuck back to my own room. I should want the same, but what I wanted most was Damien.

Or did I? Was I reacting to losing Mother and being truly alone in every world?

Not a question I'd find answers for today.

After changing clothes, I hurried to the kitchen with Zeke padding next to me. His quiet devotion shamed me. I wasn't alone, not by a longshot.

The cook was already at his station. When he saw he, he grinned. "Got your note. So glad you're here. I worried your, erm, past life might have caught up with you."

Excellent. He'd given me an excuse. I smiled back. "It did, sort of. But everything's okay now."

He nodded knowingly. "These things take time. Others often don't want us to change because it works against their interests." He cleared his throat and gestured at a pile of russet potatoes. "Start with them."

"Grated or sliced?" I grabbed an apron off the rack and tied it around my waist. Zeke curled up in his usual corner.

"You tell me," the cook replied.

"Grated. I love hash browns."

I went to work on the potatoes. Life wasn't so bad

here. Maybe Damien was wrong about our time drawing to a close.

Except, so far he hadn't been wrong about much of anything.

Live in the moment, I told myself as I grated spuds. *Live in the moment.*

It pushed the pain of losing mother to a place that didn't hurt quite so much.

"I will miss her too," Zeke told me and whined.

The cook thought he was hungry and plopped a dish of scraps down. Zeke scarfed through them and murmured, *"Like it here."*

I did too. Why was it so tough to admit? Maybe because every time I got comfortable—or thought I did—it was ripped out from under me.

CHAPTER EIGHTEEN, DAMIEN

I hadn't meant to be hard on Morgan, but I hated to see her sink into feeling sorry for herself. What happened to Zoelle was the best possible outcome. The Coven had riddled both her body and her mind with poison. That she'd been able to overcome it at the end to reach out to her daughter was a testament to her magic and her strength.

The best outcome for Zoelle, I corrected myself. Her demise booted me back into the keeping-secrets corner. Logan had reminded me again to hold silence regarding what I knew. My hopes Zoelle would fill in the blanks had died along with her.

More concerning, Zoelle's Coven knew precisely where she'd been. How had they penetrated the shielding around Faery? Either they'd grown a whole lot stronger, or we'd become weaker.

Or something else entirely was in play.

I'd suspected from the gate the Coven had joined forces with some iteration of dark sorcery. Damn near all practitioners of evil are stronger than Fae.

What I kept stumbling over was why the Coven had felt the need for such a Draconian step.

If their goal was to keep Morgan from ever finding out about her destiny, kicking her out and moving Zoelle out of the way would have accomplished it. Still, they'd signed some sort of pact with darkness to shield themselves from consequences.

Or I assumed they had.

Where would the anticipated fallout come from?

I fisted a hand but stopped shy of driving it into the nearest wall. I had many questions and painfully few answers.

How about none at all?

The day was young. Would I show up at the jobsite or return to Faery? Logan was convening an emergency council session because he was certain we hadn't seen the last of the Coven. They'd proven they could drill through our protections with magic. Following up with their bodies wouldn't take much more effort.

In all the years since the Fae were formed, and the Celts split us into dark and light segments, there's never been a battle in Faery. We've engaged in many conflicts, but always on our enemy's turf.

Our lands are delicate. Logan expressed concern

about them surviving in the face of a full-on onslaught from the Coven—or whoever was behind them driving their actions.

My fist loosened. I changed into cleaner clothes.

Morgan's scent lingered in my room; I inhaled wishing she was still here.

It was a diversion. I needed to do the right thing, which entailed stopping by the jobsite and quitting. It wasn't fair to the foreman to wonder if I'd show up each day.

If things didn't blow up in Faery, I felt certain he'd hire me back. If not him, someone would. Skilled labor was in demand, but this phase of my life was drawing to a close. Probably, there'd be no more masquerading as mortal.

Grateful to have my next moves mapped out, I directed a sliver of magic and looked in on Morgan and Zeke in the kitchen. She bent over a table chopping vegetables and chatting with the cook. Zeke rolled onto his belly, ears pricked as he sensed my presence.

"Ssht. I was never here," I told him.

His jaws split into a wolfy grin, except in this instance he wore his dog glamour. I withdrew as stealthily as I'd arrived.

If I remained long enough to eat, I could at least catch a real glimpse of Morgan, but it would slow me down. Determined to be more than a bit player in any decisions arising from today's council meeting, I gathered a spell and instructed it to spit me out a short distance from the jobsite.

I'd need to collect my tools, but it was doable. While I know how to drive, I've never wanted the hassle of owning a car. Simpler to travel my way—cheaper too. The day was just getting underway when I strolled over to the knot of men grouped around the foreman.

"Good to see you," he called in gruff tones.

A pang of guilt cut deep. He'd been decent overall, tolerant of my frequent absences. My first allegiance was to Faery, though, not a man I'd met a scant handful of months ago and would likely never see again.

I nodded in his direction. "Sorry about this, but something's come up. Family emergency. I came by to collect my tools and maybe a check for last week's work." I started to add it was okay if he didn't pay me but wisely sat on that comment. It would look suspicious and might peg me as a member of the 1 percent who didn't need wages.

The foreman disengaged himself from the group of men and strode toward me. "Can't you give me even one more day? We're at a critical juncture here. Every man is needed, and it will take me days to replace you even if I go through the registry."

By that, he meant the union. We were an odd mix of union and non-union workers. Not exactly legal since he paid us non-union types under the table.

He wasn't asking all that much. Not really, but I

couldn't be two places, and I needed to be with my kinsmen.

I smoothed over my words with a calming spell.

"I'm truly sorry, but I have a plane to catch in the middle of the day. This came up quickly. My mother fell ill. If I don't go now, I might not..."

I stopped there. Best to let him fill in the blanks.

"Sorry to hear that," the foreman mumbled. "Keep us in mind, you hear. Your last week's wages will be in the usual spot."

"Will do. Thanks for everything." I extended a hand, and we shook.

By the "usual spot," he meant a bank transfer from a shell corporation to an offshore account.

"Hey, Damien," one of the men called. "You coming back?"

I shrugged. "Hard to say. Why?"

"I'll buy your shit."

My attention snapped to the voice's owner, a tall blond man I'd been paired with several times. "Fair price?" I angled my head.

He nodded. "Of course." After a pause, he added, "Would you take four large for the lot?"

It was more than fair, and it got me out from under transporting all those heavy tools. Still, I hesitated, to make it appear I was mulling it over. "Four large plus two C notes," I said.

He pushed toward me, hand extended. "Done. Follow me. I need my phone for Venmo. It's in my truck."

Venmo, huh? I did have an account, but I hate electronic money. The Cayman Island account was a necessary evil. I'd never actually used Venmo before.

We reached a fairly new extended-cab full-ton Ford. How could he afford a truck like this? They went for close to eighty grand.

Eh, none of my business.

After unlocking the door, he reached under the seat, pulled out a wad of cash, and peeled bills off it.

I stared. "What happened to Venmo?"

"It was just for show. Don't want any of them even thinking about breaking into my ride. Good knowing you, Damien."

I pocketed the money. "Same back at ya."

After turning to walk away, I heard the door slam and the lock click. The dude who'd bought my tools—Abe something or other—must have a side gig. Likely something illegal if he ran around with that kind of cash on hand.

He'd made my life simpler, though.

I checked to make certain no one was watching me before I ducked into my favorite alley and prepped a travel spell to transport me to Faery. I'd done the right thing. Been up front about my intentions and not burned any bridges.

Before my casting took off, three sharp raps in the

vicinity of my third ear made me reel in my spell. It was Roland's signal. I hadn't exactly forgotten about the Druid, but he'd been far from the forefront of my mind. I was in a hurry to get to Faery, but not so much of one to push an information source aside.

After listening carefully, I altered my destination to the Druid guild house.

Roland was waiting in one of the gardens. A sound shield clacked around us as soon as I walked past beds of blooming roses and joined him. "Could be good timing," I told him. "I was on my way to Faery."

Rather than his usual smile, his mouth was set in grim lines. "Then I'm in time. I feared I might not be."

I waited, girding myself for bad news.

He cleared his throat. "What the Fae do is, of course, none of my affair, but you might advise your brethren to steer well clear of all witches."

I spun one hand in a get-on-with-it gesture. He didn't know what had happened to Zoelle, and I wasn't about to fill him in. No reason to.

"I don't have verification for some of this," Roland continued, "but from what I've gathered, Hecate is disappointed in both the Coven structure and her witches. She sat with her dissatisfaction until she discovered many witches had joined with Kelpies. The resulting spawn are pure evil. Over the past couple of centuries, they've quietly taken over key positions in most Covens until the 'good' witches are a minority."

I held up a hand. "You're telling me Kelpies can procreate?"

He blew out a tense breath. "Aye, 'twas a surprise to me as well. The children bear no resemblance to their sires. No way to tell by looking at them."

I absorbed the information. "Go on."

"Not much more to tell. Hecate is beyond furious. She gathered many of the other Greek gods to aid her." He stopped for a beat and narrowed his eyes. "This next is rumor, but she selected a witch to rise above the rest, to lead them out of this morass.

"Apparently, she's been planning this for hundreds of years. The Kelpie problem is old."

"So why hasn't this witch shown herself?" I asked, playing dumb.

"Not sure. Didn't get that far, but I wanted to report in." He gripped my upper arm. "Dangerous territory. You may want to steer far clear. Last time the Greek gods got involved, they mowed through everyone without bothering to check which side they were on."

I started to ask which event that had been, but it wasn't important. No one had laid eyes on any of the gods —Greek, Roman, or Celtic—for most of my long lifetime.

"You've done well," I told him. "You'll have your gold within the week."

"I'm not digging any deeper," he cautioned.

"Didn't expect you to." I tapped his hand, and he let go of me.

"Be careful," he said before walking away.

I visualized home, my mind busy. The Kelpie-linked witches had somehow caught wind of Hecate's plans. They'd been on the lookout for the witch bearing her mark. In Morgan's case, the telltale feature had to be her mismatched eyes.

Among other things, it meant the various Covens weren't the independent entities we'd assumed. They must have an established communication network. Who sat behind Kelpies? Perhaps the Fuath, a loosely established band of evil spirits roaming the Highlands. It might encompass local Covens, but what about the ones in other countries?

By the time Faery firmed up around me, I'd taken big steps toward leaving the job part of my Earth-linked life behind. My kinsmen needed me if we were going to get to the bottom of the witch problem. Roland had been anxious to spit out what he knew and establish distance between the Druids and a brewing storm.

Maeve fell into step next to me as I hurried toward the council chamber. Excellent. It meant I wasn't late. Today, she was garbed in a blood-red robe sashed in white. Something about her expression alerted me, so I asked, "What else have you scryed?"

"How do you know I saw anything?" she countered.

I shrugged. "Known you for a long time."

"Mmph. I will tell the council. No reason to repeat myself."

Surprise thrummed through me. Her comment was borderline rude, which wasn't like her. Whatever had materialized in her globe or her pool must have rattled her.

Guilt prodded. The Fae were mixed up in this mess because of my connection with Morgan—and Zeke. It might be best for all concerned if I took them and moved elsewhere.

Might be.

No guarantee Morgan would go along with my plan. She was furious with the Coven and deep into craving revenge for Zoelle's torture and death. Revenge meant up close and personal, not running for cover.

Besides, who knew when Hecate would show up and claim her own. A better question was why she'd waited this long.

We reached the large double doors leading into our council chamber. Maeve pushed past me heading for her customary spot to Logan's right at the head of a long table.

I wasn't part of the council, so I took a seat off to one side in the gallery section. Once all twelve members arrived, Logan shut and sealed the doors with magic. I felt him paint them shut.

The surprises kept on rolling. I couldn't recall a council meeting that hadn't been open to any Fae who wished to attend.

"Maeve." Logan gestured at the seer to come forward.

She stood, withdrew a crystal globe from within her robes, and blew on it. The orb lit from within. I left my seat and came closer to ensure I didn't miss anything. Logan joined me, apparently for the same reason. He'd been seated behind the sphere.

Women danced and swayed around a fire, long hair flowing around them. I assumed they were witches. One separated herself from the group and raised her arms. The others fell to their knees before her.

With no warning, the scene altered radically. The fires roared higher. The one standing dropped her arms to her sides and walked among her minions, tapping one after the other. Screams filled the council chamber as the unfortunate women marched into fire, turning into living pyres.

The orb shaded red as blood mingled with flames.

Maeve slashed the hand not supporting the sphere downward. The imagery quieted. "This is not for us," she shouted. "We make a grave error to mingle with witch politics. The one killing her own is Hecate. We must not involve ourselves."

Her ice-blue gaze bored into me.

Refusing to be cowed, I stared back. "If you're expecting me to apologize for extending aid to Morgan, you'll be waiting forever."

"Your actions arose out of goodness." Logan's tone was placating. "Surely, you understand why this falls outside the realm of Fae affairs."

What did he expect? That I was going to back down, slink away, and let Morgan sink?

I faced him. "Since when do we turn our backs on those who need us?"

"We don't when they're one of us," he shot back.

"I don't recall us making that differentiation. We've helped the Druids. We've stood with the Sidhe."

"That was different." Color rose to Logan's face. "They work white magic."

"So do witches," I reminded him. "Not all of them are evil."

Before he could contradict me, or dig himself further into his "us against them" position, I kept on talking. "Before I came here, my Druid spy caught up with me..."

Long, low whistles ran through the council room as I relayed what Roland had told me.

"That's all fine and well," Maeve said, "but this is not our war. No matter how you feel about Morgan."

"I'm not asking for your help," I replied, "although it would be in line with our covenant to stand by those in need."

"What do you want?" Logan asked, an exasperated edge lining his tone. At least he hadn't chased me out of the chamber.

I'd been thinking about it. "None of the next parts will play out quickly," I said. "If Hecate were in a hurry, she'd have made a move by now. Given the vision in Maeve's sphere, my bet is she's waiting for the witches to rise against each other to clarify who's on which side."

"When she finds out, woe betide those who've crossed her," Maeve muttered.

"Could be a good thing," I said. "Still, there's a lot of territory to cover between marching witches who've consorted with Kelpies—and their spawn—into fire and altering the existing Coven structure to allow for one witch to govern everyone."

I paused long enough to inhale and blow out a breath. "Do you still believe it's ill-advised for me to fill Morgan in on what we know?"

Maeve drew her white brows together and shot a pointed glance Logan's way. He frowned and turned his hands palms up before admitting, "She has to know. The question revolves around timing."

"May I determine when is best?" I looked from him to Maeve.

Finally, they nodded.

I extended my right arm in front of Maeve. "Release me from the blood bond."

She murmured a few words; prickles traveled from the crown of my head to my feet. The faint scarring on my forearm dissolved until only smooth flesh remained.

"Thank you." I inclined my head.

Good to have permission rather than be backed into the forgiveness corner. I could have stopped there, but I didn't. "I will leave you to your council meeting.

Hopefully, you'll find it in your hearts to be there for Morgan—and for me—if we hit a rough patch."

"If you take on every Kelpie in the Highlands, 'rough patch' will be an understatement," Maeve growled.

"Don't forget the matter of their spawn," one of the council spoke up. "They'll be protective over their own blood."

I wasn't so certain about that. If what I remembered about the Scottish water horses was accurate, they weren't even loyal to one another.

"We're a long way from a full-on Kelpie war," I reassured my kinsfolk. "I can't predict Morgan's reactions, but she might not embrace her destiny."

"What choice does she have?" Maeve pursed her lips into a disapproving moue. "None of us can sidestep what's foretold for us."

"We can rail against it, though."

Before the discussion devolved into how—and if— Fae fit into the grand scheme of prophecies and witches, I turned and walked toward the doors.

Except they were barred to me until Logan barked a word that allowed me through. The swoosh of his spell sealed them behind me.

The meeting could have been far worse. They could have amplified Maeve's original position, which was we wouldn't get involved no matter what.

If war pitted sorcery against white magic, the Fae

would fight just as we always had, but I was running ahead of the tide.

My first task was Morgan. I had a wee bit of time to sort how to approach her, but I wouldn't sugarcoat anything. She'd just lost her mother. Still, no mollycoddling.

I'd give her the facts and support her.

And love her and cherish her...

Maybe later, I answered myself. For now, my feelings, which had done nothing but deepen, would only muddy the waters.

CHAPTER NINETEEN, MORGAN

The day passed quickly between working in the kitchen and checking the streets both in front of and behind the boardinghouse to make certain no more hex bags had been scattered to nab the unwary.

Try as I might—and I thought of little else—I couldn't determine why I'd been targeted. Or Mother. She'd been a valued member of the Coven, instrumental in writing up our covenant and always hip-deep in day-to-day workings of our witch group.

Others had told me I was fortunate she was my mother.

In the lull between lunch and dinner, while walking Zeke I pushed backward in time to the day I'd first noticed she was gone. It wasn't the day she actually disappeared, just the first time I'd looked around and thought to myself it had been a while since I'd seen her.

Zeke and I were in the park a few blocks from home, the same one where he'd been held prisoner by the Coven.

"Are you all right walking through here?" I asked.

He woofed and plumed his tail.

I took it as a good sign and angled toward an empty bench set within a circle of evergreens. Trees have always been my friends. This grove would protect us. I crouched near Zeke and kept my voice low.

"Do you remember when Mother went missing?"

"Two moon cycles before the Coven said we had to leave."

I chewed my lower lip. That long. I'd been thinking it hadn't been more than a couple of weeks between when I tried to raise Mother and couldn't and the Coven showing Zeke and me the door.

"Do you know why they turned on us?"

It was a reasonable question since the familiars had their own network fueled by gossip and sometimes petty jealousies.

His shoulders slumped; his tail drooped.

"Well?" I pressed.

Familiars cannot lie, but they can withhold information.

"Not really," he growled.

I tried another tack. "Tell me everything you know."

He could refuse, but if he did it meant he had something big to hide.

He settled onto his haunches, avoiding my gaze. *"We*

will never live there again. I will not add to your misery with tales that might not be true."

I wrapped my arms around his neck, breathing in the clean animal smell of him. He leaned into me.

"I have to figure out what to do next," I told the wolf. "Tough to do when I'm working in a vacuum."

"What does that mean?" He licked the side of my face.

"My information is incomplete. Something has been brewing with the Coven for a long while. It's not all the witches, not even half of them, but a subset of the group grew distant.

"It started a long time ago, but the impact was subtle. So subtle, I paid it little heed." I hugged him tighter against me. For once, it wasn't raining, and his thick coat wasn't saturated with rainwater.

I shored up his glamour in a few spots where it flagged.

"Anything you know or have heard could help me," I pressed.

"Sita said a few things, but they mostly had to do with Zoelle."

Hearing Mother's name hurt; probably, it always would. My experience with death is limited. Not surprising coming from a group of immortals. In all my years with the Coven, there'd only been one other witch who'd passed over. I'd been very young, and no one was willing to say much beyond her mind had been destroyed by too many trips to Satan's realm.

At the time, I couldn't imagine anyone consorting with demons, so I'd pushed the episode aside. In truth, I hadn't thought about it again until now.

Zeke wasn't going to say more. I could have pushed harder, but his loyalty to me is beyond question. I had to rely on his judgment.

"Ready to go back?" I asked.

He licked my face again. I took it as a yes.

I kept my guard up on the way to the boardinghouse. No witches. No hex bags. Nothing beyond knots of mortals all intent on going somewhere.

Settling into what was becoming a familiar routine in the kitchen soothed me. Soon, Damien would be back from work—or Faery. I longed for his solid presence far more than was wise.

He'd been kind to me, but I shouldn't encourage my growing dependence on him. He had his own magical circles, far healthier ones than the Coven. While I longed to be part of Faery, I never would be. Witches have always stood alone. It would have been handy if Covens ever worked together, but they didn't. Each was its own entity.

I was aware of many others, but if I showed up at another guild house, they wouldn't welcome me. Far from it. They'd send me packing with instructions to make things right with my home Coven.

Ha. As if it would ever happen. My former sisters were out for blood.

Stop feeling sorry for yourself, an inner voice counseled gently.

Damn it. Damien had sort of said the same thing. Kind of a buck up, buttercup lecture.

I wasn't paying attention and narrowly missed chopping through a finger. My sharp intake of breath alerted the cook who glanced my way. "You okay?"

"Yeah. Fine." I returned to cutting up meat for the evening stew.

If I got off the pity pot, fury would roll in. Fuck. Why couldn't I squat on some middle ground. One less fraught with potholes. Being sunk in sorrow mired me in inaction. If I let it go, my need to avenge Mother would take over.

Burning the guild house to the ground would be satisfying, but I'd still be left with the horrid hollow sense I'd missed something critical. My mind raced in tired circles, getting me nowhere fast.

The remainder of dinner preparation passed in a blur. Soon, I was checking the dining room to make certain everyone was done eating. I must have eaten too, but I had no memory of it.

Zeke had asked to go to our room. He's perfectly capable of opening doors, but I'd made a show of ushering him up the stairs before returning to my tasks.

Damien hadn't shown up.

It shouldn't have bothered me as much as it did, but his absence was one more blow reinforcing my earlier impression I'd grown far too dependent on him. What did I know about men, anyway? Was it normal for me to long for him? Think about him all the time?

I was turning into one of those lovesick bitches on daytime TV, and I didn't care for the transition. No wonder men were banned from Covens. All they led to was trouble.

"Tomorrow will be a better day," the cook said as I was hanging up my dishtowel and apron.

I dredged up a smile. "Of course it will."

In my tiny room, I debated taking a shower. My hair was greasy, and the hot water would feel good.

Zeke jumped up from where he'd been curled on the narrow bed, tail wagging. So much for my shower idea. "You want another walk before bed?"

Ignoring me, he covered the distance to the door with his ears pricked forward.

Sluggish, slow on the uptake, I directed a thin beam of seeking magic. Lethargy departed. I threw the door open.

Damien strode through absorbing all the air in the room. Breath caught in my throat.

"Sorry I missed dinner. My, erm, meeting ran longer than expected." He kicked the door shut.

All my intentions about keeping my distance fled. I threw my arms around him and hung on as if he was the only anchor in an ocean threatening to pull me under. A sob escaped, followed by several more.

Get hold of yourself, my inner voice hissed.

He gathered me close, crooning in Gaelic. "There. There. It can't be as bad as all that."

Zeke pushed between our legs. A sound shield fell into place around us. Good. Last thing I needed was someone hearing me cry.

We stood like that for a long time before I untangled my arms. "Sorry. I'm sorry. Not sure what's wrong with me, but I'll get over it. Promise." I tried to smile but failed.

He arched a dark brow. "Really? Your entire world imploded, and you're apologizing because it's left you raw? Come on, Morgan. You're smarter than that."

"Not feeling very smart or anything else," I mumbled. At least my tears had retreated, and the pressure in my chest was more tolerable.

"Did anything happen today?" he asked.

"If you're wondering whether I have an excuse for being a maudlin mess, the answer is no. I spent far too much of today thinking. No matter how hard I tried, I couldn't figure out why the Coven wanted Mother out of the way—or why they abandoned me. What did I ever do to any of them?"

"Your mother knew things."

"But what?" I blurted. "Only thing she told me is the problem wasn't my odd eyes. Since when is 'knowing things' a death sentence?"

He gathered me close again. "I care about you. A lot.

Remember what I said about our paths crossing for a reason?"

At my nod, he went on. "I want to be part of your life, Morgan. Not because I feel sorry for you or because you need a friend."

"Then why?" My voice was muffled against his chest.

"I'm falling in love with you. You're all I think about. Magic may have thrown us together, but we found one another for a reason. It wasn't accidental you chose this boardinghouse.

"For the first time, I understand why I'd been here spinning my wheels here. I was waiting for you, though I didn't know it until you walked through the door."

My chest felt full but in a different way than it had earlier. I threaded my arms around his back letting my fingertips trail over slabs of muscle beneath his flannel shirt.

Confusion vied with a joy I had no right to feel. Mother was dead. My witch family had disowned me. My world would be bleak forever.

"Do not push him away," Zeke woofed and wriggled in his spot between us.

"Aye, don't push me away." Damien stroked hair back from my face, tucking it behind an ear. He scooped me into his arms; we ended up sitting on the bed with me in his lap.

Zeke stuck close.

"I spent most of the day in Faery." His deep voice buzzed near my ear. "Earlier, I quit my job to free up time."

"You did what?" I bolted upright. He held tight, not letting me leave. "But how will you live?"

"Faery has ample resources. I never needed outside work, but I can't sit around doing nothing."

I tried to wrap my mind around the information. "Why quit now?"

"Maeve believes we may be on the edge of a war. Faery needs me, and so do you even though you fight against it."

I could have protested, paid lip service to my independence, but both of us would have known it was a sham. I'd hugged him first. The fire that had ignited within me once I realized who stood outside my door burned too hotly to deny.

"It's a lot to take in," I murmured.

"It would be, particularly for a witch who's been taught men are anachronisms."

"When you put it that way..." I leaned into him again. "You're not feeling like an anachronism."

"Fess up. Bet there have always been witches who stepped outside the bounds of your rules."

I nodded. "So long as children didn't result, the Coven mostly looked the other way."

Damn. The further I got from Coven structure, the

more hypocritical it appeared. Why had I not seen it earlier?

"Because you weren't looking. It was all you knew." Damien had obviously been inside my head.

"Wish you wouldn't do that," I mumbled.

"Sorry. It's second nature." He tipped my chin with a forefinger. "What do you want?"

"Normal," I blurted. "Except it will never happen."

"No, it won't," he agreed. "Not the old normal, but you can forge a new one. Might be better than what you're longing for."

Before I could respond, he covered my mouth with his. The kiss was gentle, tentative. It offered choices. I could pull away.

I should pull away. My plate was overflowing. Last thing I needed was an ill-timed romance.

What did I know about romance or timing? Perhaps no relationship ever began under auspicious circumstances.

His lips enticed. Firm yet gentle as he pressed them against mine. I wound my arms around his shoulders and fell headlong into my first kiss. Unlike some of my sisters, I'd never been tempted to lift my robes for any mortal. I'd been too busy cataloging fauna and flora and making corrections in our long-term logbooks.

My task had grown more complex as species died out in a warming world. Then I'd been truly absorbed in worry. Witches are guardians of the natural world. Until the sisterhood captured Mother, I'd never have imagined them capable of such a gesture.

And then I stopped thinking.

Sensation engulfed me. The scents of the outdoor world swirled, saltwater and wet evergreens. I moved from accepting his kiss to kissing him back. Awareness rolled through me highlighting everything at once. The press of his chest against my breasts. His fingers threated into my hair. His mouth busy against mine. When he licked the seam between my lips, I opened my mouth to his tongue. My breath quickened.

Every cell came alive, alight with need; my heart jumped to triple-time rhythm.

I wasn't unfamiliar with sex, but it had always been a solitary pursuit. Like scratching a persistent itch. Once it was over, I'd retreated to whatever I'd been occupied with before.

Being held, kissed, and caressed was as different as night from day. I explored the planes of Damien's body, wanting to memorize every nuance. He ran his lips across my cheekbone to my ear and then down my neck. My nipples hardened against his chest. Every movement sliding our bodies together intensified my delight.

And my need.

He lifted his mouth from my neck. "Didn't mean to do that." His deep voice had a catch in it. "But you're irresistible."

The place he'd been pressed against me felt cold. "Don't stop," I murmured and wriggled closer.

"I don't want to." He touched my lips with a finger. "But we need to talk. Depending on the outcome of that conversation, we'll make plans."

His words cut through the pleasurable bubble around me like a bucket of icy water. For the first time today, I'd stepped beyond my sorrow and confusion. My break from reality was over.

"What kind of plans?"

"Depends on you." He lifted me off his lap and dragged the room's only chair across from the bed. Once he'd settled into it—the flimsy wood creaking beneath his bulk—he said, "No easy way to share any of this, so I'm just going to throw things out there."

Zeke, who'd moved near the window when Damien was kissing me, sat by my side. I tucked my legs beneath me.

"Do not tell her," the wolf said to Damien.

I stared at my familiar. The desire and joy I'd felt in Damien's arms receded to a dull ache. Zeke did know something—maybe a whole lot. But he'd chosen to keep me in the dark.

"I have to," Damien replied. "She deserves to know."

"But it will hurt her, and there's nothing she can do about it."

"We believe there is," Damien replied. By "we" he must mean the Fae.

I buried a hand in Zeke's thick fur. He loved me and had done his best to spare me from disturbing news. I couldn't fault him for it.

"It will be all right. Just get on with whatever this is," I told him. Or maybe I was saying it to them both.

Damien's green gaze skewered me. "It has to be because you can't change any of it."

The tight ball that had curled my innards into a knot was back. How could I be hundreds of years old and so unprepared for anything beyond my usual sphere?

Not that I had a usual anything any longer.

I laced my fingers together and met Damien's direct gaze. "Tell me whatever this is. The sooner I know, the sooner I can figure out what to do next."

Zeke pushed closer, protecting me with his body.

A chill shuffled down my spine followed by several more.

Nothing is worse than not knowing, though. I wanted to drag the truth from Damien, but care shone from his eyes. He scooted close, took one of my hands in his, and started talking.

"I don't have all the details, but it appears Hecate intervened long ago when it came to her attention not all her witches were honest and aboveboard. Some wielded dark power..."

I wanted it to be a lie, but incontrovertible truth pinged off his words. My life would be forever changed in the next few minutes, but those alterations had their roots deep in history.

Finally the answers I'd sought were about to surround me.

At least there'd be answers. No matter how much I resented them, knowledge was power.

Or it could be if I acted decisively and didn't make too many mistakes.

CHAPTER TWENTY, DAMIEN

I shouldn't have kissed Morgan, shouldn't have held her tight. Letting go so I could impart knowledge she should have known long since was one of the hardest things I've ever done. If I'd followed my heart, I'd have taken her and Zeke to a special world not far from Faery where we could have lived many a long year without anyone finding us.

Still, her destiny would have caught up eventually. She'd have been furious when she discovered I'd known all along and hidden things from her. Relationships cannot begin on lies, not ones with any hope of lasting.

Morgan was important to me. More important than renegade witches. More important than Hecate's long-simmering revenge. More important than potentially involving my kin in a war.

That last made me wince. My first allegiance should be to the Fae, but it wasn't.

Instead, I'd prioritized shielding Morgan, cherishing her, protect her. Failing that, I'd stand by her side and slay any who threatened her existence. It would toss Hecate and me into the same court as allies. I had no idea how the witch goddess felt about Fae, but if she were wise, she'd accept help where it was offered.

"Damien? There must be more." Morgan's voice dragged me out of my thoughts. After my lead-in about Hecate, I'd stopped to gather the few facts I had and organize them into a cohesive whole.

I squeezed her hand. "Aye, there is, but some is inferred from context. The probable reason our healers couldn't detect shared blood between you and your mother is because Hecate created you and swapped you for whatever child your mother carried.

"None of the Coven witches would have suspected. Zoelle was pregnant and gave birth. No reason to question the resultant child."

"It would be possible," Morgan agreed, "since we birth our few young in forest glades with our familiars in attendance." Her eyes widened. "Sita knew all along."

Zeke woofed.

She'd confided in him. "Did she tell anyone else?" I asked the wolf.

"No. Zoelle and I swore her to secrecy because we were worried about Morgan's safety."

"You weren't there until my moon blood began to flow," Morgan reminded him.

"*You dreamed me long afore that. And I had many a conversation with your mother and Sita.*" He paused before adding, "*The witch goddess chose me as your familiar.*"

"You met Hecate?" Morgan's dark brows shot up.

Zeke nodded. "*Once.*"

"It's one more time than she's shown herself to me," Morgan muttered.

"Meanwhile," I went on, "the witches in league with sorcery must have gotten wind something was up, so they searched for clues. When years passed and no one derailed their plans, they relaxed their guard."

"What plans?" Morgan asked.

"I'm not sure. We're entering conjecture at this point. The witches aligned with darkness kept it a secret. What they told the others was one witch had been marked by Hecate to pick up the reins of leadership, not only for your Coven but for them all."

"But it's ridiculous," Morgan sputtered. "We've never had any type of royalty. Covens are self-governing via a council structure not unlike yours."

"The urban myth," I went on, "was it would be dangerous for the witch leader to come to power. Bloody wars would ensue. Peace would elude every Coven. Far better to root out Hecate's chosen one and destroy her."

Morgan pinched the bridge of her nose between her

thumb and forefinger. "It sort of makes sense now. Some of it."

I made beckoning motions. "Which parts?"

"Mirabelle and them must have suspected Mother. Maybe she slipped up. Perhaps one of our healers determined she and I weren't blood linked. Once she was gone—and I'm ashamed I didn't notice for weeks or longer—my decision to drop my glamour played right into their hands.

"My odd eyes must have shocked the sisterhood, particularly in light of the witch-ruler rumors I'd never heard about."

"Why not dump you where they were holding Zoelle?"

Morgan showed me a mouthful of teeth. "Because she and I together could have joined our magic and escaped. At least we could have if I'd reached her in time. The witch we rescued was so depleted, she was beyond fighting back."

"Keep in mind," I said, "most of your Coven had no idea Zoelle had been kidnapped. Remember, we didn't find witches standing guard. Banshees and a Dearg. No matter what story Mirabelle ginned up, surely Coven justice would have played out differently."

"Yes. We've never tortured our own." Bitterness lined Morgan's words.

She slid her hand from under mine and clasped both in her lap. "Some of this doesn't make sense. If I'm

Hecate's chosen, why hasn't she appeared in a dream or something? If she had a task for me, surely, she'd have told me about it."

"Unless she was waiting to make certain she'd identified all the witches who signed on with evil."

"A thankless task. She'd be waiting forever. My other question," Morgan said, "is why some witches joined up with dark magic."

"That one's simple. To gain power. We've even had the occasional Fae who signed a pact with demonspawn."

"I guess, except none of the witches I've known have been particularly motivated by world dominion. For one thing, our magic sits toward the bottom of the totem pole."

Zeke nudged her thigh with his snout.

Morgan closed her teeth over her lower lip. "Is there more?"

"The Fae council is concerned the Coven will exact revenge, except it will be tough for them to manage without revealing they'd captured Zoelle in the first place."

"Not necessarily," Morgan said. "They could lie and say the Fae abducted and killed one of their own."

"Anyone who knows aught about the Fae would see it for the lie it was." Indignation rustled through me. "We'd never have captured a witch for no reason, held her prisoner, tortured and killed her."

Morgan unclasped her hands and laid one over mine.

"You know that, but most witches haven't spent any time studying other types of magic wielders."

"Regardless of how the sisterhood spun things," I said, "what do you want to do about all of this?"

A corner of her mouth twisted downward. "Run like hell. Except it's scarcely an option."

"It is," I spoke slowly, "but eventually fate will catch up with you."

"The longer I wait," she said, "the more time the Coven will have to spin a web of lies behind my back."

It was true, but she didn't need agreement from me. She was doing fine on her own. If Hecate formed her, Morgan had the raw materials for whatever lay ahead.

Leaving the narrow bed, she paced in a tight circle. "I want to confront the Coven, but it's not smart."

"Not on your own."

Grinding to a halt, she faced me. "I have to find Hecate. She's the lynchpin in all this, the reason for my existence. Surely, she knows Mother is dead and the Coven is out for my blood."

"Maybe."

"What does that mean?" she gritted.

I pushed to my feet and stood across from her. "I'm scarcely an expert on gods or goddesses, but time flows differently for them. She could be many worlds away. If she'd been in a hurry to utilize you, she'd have shown up before now."

"But where is she?" Morgan waved a fist in the air. "I

resent being a fucking pawn in a board game I didn't know shit about until a few minutes ago."

Wrapping my arms around her, soothing her, wouldn't be wise. I'd been expecting anger and bitterness. Morgan would have to work through them.

"How about plans for now?" I kept my voice neutral.

"Huh? What plans? I have no life. It's been laid out for me since I was born, er made."

"Or maybe you're just now coming into the beginning of your full power."

I dropped a hand onto her shoulder. "We can't remain here. Well, we could, but it's not wise."

"Why not?"

"The Coven knows where you are."

"They can find me no matter where I go."

I shook my head. "I don't think so. Not if we're careful."

Her chin snapped up. "You can leave. Cut your losses. I'm not even a good bet for myself."

So much for keeping my distance, letting her work through her angst. I closed my arms around her. She wriggled, but I held tight. "I love you. I am not going anywhere. We'll see this through together."

"How do the Fae feel about it?" Her voice was muted against my chest.

"They'll always be there for me—and us. They took your mother in, didn't they?"

I purposefully didn't add anything about the "not our

way" conversation that had played out. If it came down to it, the Fae would do the right thing. My people would never stand by while evil roamed free.

She ducked from beneath my embrace. "Accepting your help doesn't feel right. I don't know how I feel about you." Color stained her cheeks. "That didn't come out right. I care about you, am grateful to you, but I have no experience with men or how we move from the newness between us to something that has longevity."

"We'd be learning together. I've never taken a mate."

"I just don't know. If something bad happened to you —" A muted sob choked off her words.

"It won't. The Coven can't hurt me. They wouldn't be that stupid. Zoelle was different. She was one of their own."

"You can't know any of that. The Coven's gone off the deep end. How will I ever know whom I can trust?"

"Let's take this a step at a time. Our first move should be leaving here for a safer spot. Once we're situated, I like your idea about trying to raise Hecate."

"Any ideas about how to actually finesse it?"

"No, but Maeve might. And if she doesn't, she'll point us in a fertile direction."

"*We should go with him.*" Zeke was on his feet, tail pluming.

Morgan turned to her familiar. "Why?"

"*It's the avenue that opened for us. Much like this place*" —he pawed at the floor—"*was there when we needed it.*"

I silently blessed Zeke. Morgan might listen to him. Words splashed the back of my throat. I sat on them. I didn't want her to feel I was pressuring her.

She returned to pacing.

Zeke's ears pricked. He ran to the window and put his paws on the ledge. I felt witches even before he growled.

Morgan spun and joined Zeke, pulling the sash to open the window. Power swirled around her; lightning bolts jetted from her fingertips finding their marks.

I stared out the opening, dialing in my third eye. Five witches were pinned to the pavement, blood pouring from their mouths.

"You will pay for what you did to Mother and for your alliance with evil," she shouted in mind speech so loud it made my head ache.

"I know about you and your filth and your plans. I will make certain everyone else knows too. You will be outcast. Pariahs."

The witches writhed. Their spirits hovered above their bodies, on the verge of breaking free.

"You're killing them," I warned.

Enchantment poured from her. "I don't care. I wish the whole bloody fucking lot of them were dead. It won't bring Mother back, but they won't get away with what they've done."

A distant siren blared. We were running out of time. Someone must have heard the witches squealing and called 911.

I pulled the window shut.

Morgan turned on me. "I wasn't done."

"Yeah, you were. They're dead. We have to get out of here now. The authorities will be here soon."

"They can't be dead. I only wanted to hurt them."

"You killed them. We can sort out how you managed it later. Grab everything that's yours."

A shell-shocked look was replacing the fury that had danced around her. She emptied the drawer with her few belongings.

"Take everything. Don't leave so much as a hairbrush."

"What about your things?"

"I'll come back for them."

Clothing spilled from her arms. I took some of it and a notebook and set a travel spell in motion. By now the sirens were right on top of us as police cars converged in the street.

The last thing I did before igniting my spell was to cleanse the chamber of Morgan's magic. It was thick in the room from her meltdown.

I aimed for a deserted cabin in the southern Cascade Range. I'd holed up here a time or two when I needed thinking space. No roads led in or out. It shaped up around us in a matter of minutes.

Morgan fired a mage light. It glowed a soft white. "Where are we?"

"Still on Earth. Only a couple of hundred miles from Seattle. Stay put."

"Where are you going?" She waved a hand my way. "Never mind. I'll be here. Zeke too."

"I'm going to get my things from the boardinghouse and check on what the cops are doing. Need to clear out the remnants of your energy—and mine—from the boardinghouse. Shouldn't be gone more than half an hour or so."

"Could you leave the cook a note?" Morgan fished the notebook out from under her stack of garments.

"Not the wisest move," I told her.

"He was kind. I don't want him to worry."

Finally, I nodded. "Okay. No details."

She scratched something on the top sheet of paper, tore it out, and handed it to me.

Appreciate your kindness. I have to leave. Don't worry about me. Everything is fine.

"Looks good." My voice was gruff. Morgan's soft edges were endearing. How many would be left a month from now? Or a year?

"I'll watch over her," Zeke woofed.

"Thanks." I ruffled his fur and walked through the portal I hadn't closed off.

Back in my room, I gathered what I wanted to keep, leaving the rest for whoever inhabited this chamber next. I scattered power to obliterate any trace of Morgan throughout the building. A glance out the window revealed ambulances, flashing lights, and a host of emergency workers and lookie-loos.

The Coven would put two and two together. If they hadn't been out for blood before, they would be now.

Leaving hadn't just been smart; it was our only move. We wouldn't remain in the cabin. Neither could we go to Faery. I'd have to choreograph our next steps carefully to keep Morgan safe from retribution.

Except, it wasn't looking as if she needed me to do that. The critical mass of magic pouring from her had shocked me. Witch power, yet far more.

What was she?

Did it even matter? She could morph into Medusa, and I'd still love her.

One thing was certain, though—she had to develop control over her ability. Killing because she wanted to was one thing. Killing because her emotions got away from her quite another.

She'd denied murdering the witches, seemed stunned when I reiterated the information.

Locating Hecate loomed large. If anyone could entrain her newly awakened magic, it was the witch goddess who'd created her.

Before leaving the boardinghouse, I slipped Morgan's note beneath the kitchen door. The cook would find it first thing the next morning.

Except he must have been inside because the swinging door slammed against its stops as he hurried out. I girded myself for anything including wiping his mind. I'd erase a whole lot more than Morgan and me, but it couldn't be helped.

He clutched the note in a ham-sized hand. "Take care of her."

His reaction surprised me. "I will."

He lowered his voice. "The two of you are...different. I sense shit like that."

Oh-oh. I readied a small thread of magic to derail his memories.

"It's why I helped her," he went on. Power of his own bloomed around him. For a moment, he grew taller, broader before subsiding to his usual form.

"She was grateful," I said before walking out of the darkened dining room with the scents of his magic swirling around me.

Apparently, I wasn't the only mage set to watch over Morgan.

Hecate's hand had to be deep in this, stirring the pot.

Or not. Magic calls to its own. Hecate might not have anything to do with it.

I walked through the portal and into the cabin. Morgan and Zeke were curled on the single cot fast asleep. This time, I took care to seal my gateway so no one could follow us.

Tomorrow would be here soon enough. I placed the clothes and other items I'd rescued from my room on a table and sank into a worn leather chair. Come morning, we'd move again. Hopefully to a spot more auspicious to locating Hecate or another of her fellow gods. If we found any of the Greek contingent, they'd probably know where their kin resided.

I flicked my fingers at Morgan and Zeke, deepening their slumber. Protectiveness surged. I'd do whatever it took to see this through to its end. Morgan's notebook lay near her. I picked it up and began jotting ideas for where we could hole up while we searched for Hecate.

When Morgan woke, we'd go through the list and decide together. I'd heavied up about needing to get the hell out of the boardinghouse, but from here on we'd operate as a team.

My pen had been still for a while because I was lost gazing at Morgan. Would she still want me once she discovered the full scope of her power?

I chose to believe she would and returned to fleshing out locations we could set up shop, places we wouldn't constantly be looking over a shoulder.

"How long have you been back?" she asked in a sleep-saturated voice.

"Long enough. Feel like making plans?"

She rose, careful not to disturb Zeke, and settled into my lap. I wrapped my arms around her, lost in the moment. Our discussion could wait, not forever, but long enough for me to kiss her again and savor her nearness.

CHAPTER TWENTY-ONE,
HECATE

Cobwebs brushed her face and tangled in her long black hair. Or maybe it had turned silver in the intervening years. No mirrors in her cave. She reached for her hair, intent on running her fingers through it.

And hit the end of the chains that bound her.

Everything came flooding back. It always did, but before she could do anything to free herself, she'd fall asleep again.

Hecate made a grab for anger. It eluded her. Whoever had imprisoned her didn't want her to access any emotion that might aid in achieving freedom.

Damn Hermes. Or maybe Persephone or even Hera. Someone found out she'd meddled in witch matters, creating a child from her own essence and swapping it for one of the witch spawn.

The other babe found a decent home. It wasn't as if she'd murdered it, although she'd toyed with the idea. It would have been cleaner to not leave loose ends. As a compromise, she'd made the babe deaf and dumb and stripped its immortality.

Chains clanked as she strained against them.

Was this when she'd finally break free?

Not if I don't do something different.

Her mind was sluggish, muddy. How long had she been here? From the piles of bones scattered about, it had to be a long time. The child she'd made must be long since grown.

Was she safe, or had the Coven discovered her secret and banished her?

Hecate never would have guessed how simple it was for her fellow Greeks to lure and bind her. She'd trusted them, told them her secrets and her fears for the witches who worshipped her.

Dark rivers flowed through several Covens. If she didn't intervene, still more witches would fall to evil. She'd had a plan, and a damned good one. Create a witch in her own image, one whose magic was far stronger than usual.

That witch would see through wickedness and weed it from every Coven. When she was done, the other witches would bow to her as their queen.

Aye, the plan had been simplicity itself, but she'd needed to be present to ensure its success.

Yet, here she moldered.

Someone left food from time to time, and refilled the waterskins. She never saw a soul, so they must sneak in like thieves while she slept.

Her mind was wandering again. If she didn't take care, sleep would overtake her. Who knew when she'd waken again. Her gaze snapped to the nearest pile of bones. That had to be it. They were poisoning her.

If she quit eating, her mind would clear, her strength would return, and she'd break out of the shackles. That anyone could bind her with iron was a sick joke. Iron might hold lesser deities, but not her.

Her eyelids grew heavy. She fought the sensation. Pushed back desperately. If she could only ride out one of these waves, she'd have it. Starving herself held other penalties. She'd grow weak.

There'd be a nexus where she was too feeble to escape even if the levels of whatever they were poisoning her with retreated.

She fisted a hand; the iron band tightened around her wrist. It hurt, but pain would keep her awake.

She hoped.

All the work she'd done, all her carefully laid plans would be for naught if she couldn't get out of this cave.

My cave, she corrected herself sourly. Her kin had boobytrapped her home.

How dare they?

Drowsiness retreated a notch or two.

Was she onto something?

If she kept thinking, kept plotting revenge, would it allow her to push past the haze coating her mind?

Hecate squeezed her fist tighter and then added the other one. The thin iron bands cut into her flesh.

Blood. If only she could access hers, it would change everything. Why hadn't she thought about it before?

Because I always went back to sleep.

Why wasn't she sleeping now?

Before she got sidetracked back into dreamland, she scooted over until one wrist hovered over a sharp bone fragment. It took a few tries, but she managed to stabilize the rib bone with her body and stab the end through her wrist.

The heady, coppery smell of blood swirled.

"Coat the iron. Break the iron," she chanted over and over.

The light in the cave was dim, so she summoned a mage light, surprised when it flared blue-white. Her earlier attempts hadn't been nearly this robust.

Encouraged, she wriggled around until her other wrist was in position and stabbed it too. Rivulets flowed down her palms and fingers, wetting the ground.

Power thrummed beneath her breastbone.

"That's more like it," she muttered and went back to chanting.

The earth beneath her came alive at the touch of her blood, almost as if it had missed her. Slowly, lazily, one manacle cracked. Hecate didn't lose any time jerking her arm free. The other one took longer. She smeared blood all over the metal and summoned fire before it, too, shattered.

She tottered to her feet, shockingly weak.

It's what happened to muscles that hadn't been used in centuries.

Was she strong enough to leave?

If she did, where would she go?

"Never mind any of that." Her voice was dry, brittle, rusty from disuse.

While blood still dripped, she walked the perimeter of her cave, marking it and sealing it against entry. No more poisoned food. No visitors period. Not until she was ready to face the world again.

Her next stop was a small underground lake. Its enchanted waters rose over her head. Clean and starting to recover, she opened a chest and extracted a black robe embroidered with golden runes. It was her favorite, and the chest had kept it from crumbling to dust.

As ready as she could make herself, she ducked into the alcove with her magical bowl. The water yielded images, and she bent over it asking for news of the mage she hadn't laid eyes on since she was born.

At first, the surface remained stubbornly opaque.

Hecate didn't give up. She hadn't come this far to fail.

Her magic was as rusty as everything else, but she kept poking and prodding and pushing.

With no warning, the water sloshed from side to side. In its center, a raven-haired mage leaned out a window. Lethal power flew from her hands, dealing death to a gaggle of witches. Hecate bent closer, searching.

Yes! The eyes were unmistakable. It was how she'd marked her creation.

A wolf with the same eyes stood by her side. Ah yes. She'd made him too, but forgotten until this very moment.

From out of nowhere, a Fae joined them.

"Noooo," Hecate screeched until she realized he was friend, not foe.

Odd. Since when had the Fae befriended witches?

She held the bowl tight until the imagery played itself out. Five witches lay dead. Her witch, the one she'd sacrificed so much for, left along with her familiar and the Fae.

Hecate's lips split in a feral grin. She needn't have worried about her creation. The witch was more than capable.

Of course, she was. It was how Hecate crafted her.

But the best news was, she wasn't too late. Once she showed up, the Fae could go back to Faery. She and her minion would remake every Coven, mow through witches who'd turned their backs on white magic, and set things right in the witch world.

Hecate placed the bowl on a low shelf and rubbed her hands together in anticipation.

She couldn't wait, but she'd have to be careful until her full strength returned. If what she'd seen in her scrying bowl was accurate—and it had to be—she and her minion could burn down worlds. When they were done fixing the twisted Covens, she'd plot her revenge on those who'd decided the best place for her was in her cave imitating Sleeping Beauty.

They'd pretend it had been a joke, but she knew better.

She'd get even if it was the last thing she did.

Apologies for the mini cliff ending, but *Bound by Shadows* is one long book split into three episodes.

Scarred set the stage for Morgan and Damien's slow burn romance. It also marks Morgan's fledgling steps accepting her birthright. *Cursed*, next up in the trilogy, will be a wakeup call for Hecate. She may have located her minion, but said minion isn't the compliant accomplice the goddess expects. Neither is Damien about to "run on back to Faery."

I'd love it if you could leave a review for *Scarred*. Do it now while it's fresh in your mind and let others know what you loved about it. Thanks in advance. Doesn't need to be fancy. A line or two will do.

Read on for a sample from *Cursed*.

BOOK DESCRIPTION: CURSED

Magic runs strong in me, but power isn't enough.

I've traveled a long road since the Coven kicked me out. It's only been a matter of weeks, but it may as well be years. I've learned a lot, and nothing at all. One thing's for certain: my life up until now has been a sham.

My wolf, beloved familiar, knew far more than he disclosed. Hard to fault him since he was trying to keep me safe. Mother, the one witch who could have shed light on my origins, is dead.

Try as I might, I couldn't save her.

Along the way, a Fae took me under his wing, but it's confusing. Damien says he loves me. I have no idea what I feel beyond sorrow and anger. All I want is to torch the Coven guild house, avenge Mother's death, and locate Hecate, goddess of witches.

Secrets of my origins lie within her. Secrets forged

centuries ago. At one time, I was important to her, critical enough to bend rules.

She's abandoned me too, except she doesn't get to walk away.

I will find her and demand answers.

Answers to shape the rest of my existence.

CHAPTER ONE, MORGAN

Zeke, white wolf and beloved familiar, pranced by my side. We'd taken advantage of a rare sunny afternoon in the Pacific Northwest to stretch our legs and soak in the beauty of the natural world.

Witches are its guardians, or I thought we were.

Regardless how many of my erstwhile witch sisters have slid off the rails, I still value every plant, every animal, every crystal, every rock.

With a sideways leap, Zeke pounced and surfaced with something small and wriggling clamped between his jaws. A few crunches and it disappeared down his gullet.

"Whoa. Slow down," I teased. "What is that? Number ten?"

"Twelve," he informed me solemnly. *"Who knows when the hunting will be this plentiful again."*

It was true. Damien, a Fae who'd been in the right place at the right time to keep my world from turning into a total shitshow, was on the hunt for where we could hole up for a while. Our current location, a rustic cabin in the southern Cascade Range, wouldn't do for more than a night or two. No heat beyond a stone hearth. No food. No bedding.

Not that we couldn't procure the latter two, but Damien was convinced we could do better.

Zeke finished swallowing. *"You were different,"* he said.

I slowed and glanced at him. He's a big guy, close to 150 pounds of solid muscle with almond-shaped eyes, one amber and one white just like mine.

"Different when?"

"When you were killing all those witches."

His words sat like stones between us. I kept walking. "Didn't realize I'd gone that far," I told him. "Only meant to teach them a lesson for spying on us and scattering their dirty, nasty hex bags around. Besides, witches are supposed to be immortal. It never occurred to me I could kill them even if I'd wanted to."

"Your magic is different." He qualified his earlier statement.

This time I stopped dead. "Even now?"

Zeke flopped his head up and down. *"Go ahead. Test it."*

Wasting magic went against my principles. Unless I had a solid use for my skills, I kept them under wraps.

"We could teleport back to the cabin." His gaze zeroed in on mine.

The sun skirted the western horizon. It would be dark soon. I'd had such a pleasant time exploring a new area—one with no witches or mortals—I'd lost track of time.

I hadn't actually deployed my ability since the debacle outside the boardinghouse. By the time Damien scooted us out of there, the street had been saturated with police, ambulances, and the dreaded PDA wagon. I'd never given much thought to the Paranormal Detective Agency when I lived with my Coven—

Oh-oh, not mine any longer, I corrected myself.

Back to the PDA. It's staffed by mages, according to Damien. Meant they had power of their own and tracking skills. Before we'd left, Damien scoured my room and the rest of the lodging of any trace of my magic.

Even if he hadn't, PDA mages would have to be hella strong magically to find me all the way out here.

"Well?" Zeke nudged me with his snout..

It wasn't a bad suggestion. We were still miles from the cottage. I hadn't planned well, but the past days had been so stressful, the break had been welcome. Given a do-over, I'd probably repeat my actions.

I gathered the makings of a transport spell and visualized the small wooden structure Damien had taken us to the previous night. Zeke leaned against me to make it easy to include him.

All the pieces jumped to my command. Unusual, but not unheard of. I kindled my casting. Results were instantaneous. One moment, we stood in the forest. The next we were in front of our destination.

Breath swooshed from me; I sank to a crouch.

"See?" Zeke's tail plumed. He padded to a nearby creek and drank deeply.

No. I did not "see." Magic had been a constant all my long life. Suddenly, I was stronger by a factor of maybe five.

Or even ten.

I'd barely thought my transport spell, and here we were.

Damien had been right about me taking care slinging magic about until I had a much better handle on my newfound talent.

After pushing to my feet, I trudged up the steps deep in thought. I'd build a fire and do my damnedest to sort through this new development. Annihilating the witches should have been a wakeup call, but I'd been too wrapped up in retribution for Mother's death to think much about it.

After today's demonstration, I couldn't sidestep the issue any longer.

Some event—Mother's death?—had yanked the brakes off my magic and catapulted me into a whole new realm. One where I was stronger than any other witch living or dead.

As someone who'd always kept to herself, the concept of being thrust into any kind of limelight made me uncomfortable. Yet, if Damien were to be believed, and he had no reason to lie to me, I was some kind of latter day witch queen formed by Hecate to deliver the sisterhood from evil.

I worked automatically, gathering wood and lighting a fire, with my thoughts a tumultuous riot.

Zeke's never been the "I told you so" type. He followed me inside the cabin and curled up near the fire. When I finally settled into a worn leather chair, I wasn't any closer to finding answers.

It had been dark for a couple of hours, and I'd fed my fledgling fire a few times, before I started wondering where Damien was. His association with me was dangerous for him.

Fae are ancient, but not particularly strong magically.

Had he run into trouble? Did he need my help?

I chewed my lower lip and stared at the rise and fall of the flames. My stomach growled. Zeke had feasted, but my last meal had been the previous day.

"Want me to hunt you a couple of rabbits?" Zeke asked sleepily. He must have heard my stomach rumbling.

"Sure. Um, no. I'll live. I'm worried about Damien."

Zeke wasn't quite on his feet, but he'd rolled onto his belly.

"When did he say he'd be back?"

"He didn't, but he's been gone maybe fifteen hours. It's a long time."

"If we leave and he comes here, he'll worry," the wolf pointed out.

"I can leave him a note. But my intent is to track him. Means we'd locate him before he returned to this spot."

I stood and walked toward the door.

"Where are you going?" If Zeke had been truly concerned, he'd have joined me. His overly full tummy was calling the shots. He'd stand beside me, but only if I needed his protection.

"I'm going to deploy seeking magic. Easier from outdoors."

"Do not leave without me." Zeke was back curled in a ball.

"No worries on that front. I'll be in the yard."

I grabbed my coat off a hook and snugged into it. The evening was chilly, and this way I wouldn't squander magic keeping warm. I passed the bottom step and faced away from the house.

Eyes closed, I sought Damien's unique magical signature. All mages have them. At first, nothing pinged off my casting. Had too many hours passed? Should I have done this midday instead of traipsing off on a carefree hike?

Try harder, an inner voice urged.

Duh. What choice did I have? To leave here in search

of Damien meant I needed a ballpark idea about where he'd gone. Failing that, I could rattle Faery's gates and see if anyone would show up and let me inside.

Since I'm not Fae, I cannot penetrate the veils separating Fae lands from Earth. At one point, Damien had said he'd see about fixing that problem and allowing me access, but he wouldn't have had time with everything else that had transpired.

Back to "try harder."

I cycled through every element and every direction experimenting with different combinations. Occasionally, I'd get a faint hit, but it eluded me when I tried to glom onto it.

It finally occurred to me that he'd masked his movements.

Did he not want me following him?

A glance at the stars and half moon suggested it was pushing midnight. Waiting here forever wasn't wise. Zeke and I would survive, but I couldn't stand not knowing where Damien was.

I clumped back up the steps. The fire was reduced to a glowing bed of coals. No point in feeding it.

Zeke opened one eye. *"That took a while."*

"Because nothing worked for me."

"Do you want to look for him?"

I nodded. "Problem is where to start. He didn't share his plans."

The wolf got to his feet and shook himself from head

to tail tip. *"We can go to Faery. Surely, they have a way of keeping track of their people."*

"I can't get in. Not without Damien or Logan or one of the Fae," I reminded him.

Zeke's tail swished from side to side. *"I can. I'll mind link with Sita."*

"Perfect. Why didn't I think of that?" Bending, I hugged his furry head.

"Because you're not a familiar."

State the obvious, why don't you. Sita was a hawk. She'd been Mother's bird and was devastated by her death. Since she couldn't return to the Coven and witches who'd tortured and killed her bondmate, she'd chosen to remain in Faery.

I took stock of the few things in the cabin. Garments, my notebook, and a few of Damien's magical accoutrements. They'd be safe enough, but I stacked and folded and layered protection spells over everything.

It didn't take long.

"We're ready," I told the wolf.

He followed me down the steps.

The cottage lacked a lock, so I sealed it with magic. If anyone tried to enter—unlikely since no roads led to this location—they'd encounter a hell of a shock.

After visualizing the place I'd crossed into Faery the times I'd been there, I loosed my spell. Just as before, the transition was so fast it stole my breath. I'd been about to nudge Zeke into action, but he'd already deployed telepathy calling Sita.

Not sure what I'd been expecting, but Maeve and Logan appeared immediately. Sita rode on Maeve's shoulder, but made a beeline for Zeke. They'd been friends when Mother and I were still part of the Coven.

"Thanks for coming so quickly," I began.

"Took you long enough," Maeve snapped. One of the Fae seers, she was tall, gaunt, and garbed in a black robe sashed in red. White hair fell to shoulder level and she skewered me with ice-blue eyes.

"We've been expecting you for hours," Logan added. Head of the Fae council, he was about Maeve's height with gobs of blond curls. Almond shaped silver eyes stared at me. A blue robe hung off his shoulders half covering black trousers.

Why oh why do the fucking Fae always put me on the defensive?

"Damien told me to wait for him," I said. "When it grew later and later, I tried to track him and couldn't. So we came here. Why were you expecting me sooner? What do you know? Is Damien all right?"

Once the questions started, I couldn't stem the flow.

Magic glowed around Zeke and Sita as they communicated telepathically.

"Do you suppose it's safe to let her in?" Logan exchanged a pointed glance with Maeve.

Magic began at the crown of my head scouring me. It burned and stung, but I held still.

"Aye," Maeve replied. "She had naught to do with this."

"With what?" I shouted, sick of them treating me much as the Coven had, like a miscreant and outcast.

Not that I was one of the Fae, but we'd fought together. Surely, it counted for something. Comrades in arms and all that rot.

"Follow us," Logan instructed.

"Not safe to talk out here," Maeve added.

The veils parted; the Fae stepped through along with Zeke and Sita. I hesitated, but not for long. If I blew Maeve and Logan off, they'd probably never open Faery to me again.

Seething and worried sick, I plodded through just in time for one of the veils to clip my backside as it fell into place.

"Ouch," I muttered. How could a thing that looked so diaphanous pack such a punch?

"Your own fault," Logan said without looking back.

"Be quicker next time." Maeve's rebuke piled on the heels of his rankled.

"*They know something,*" Zeke spoke into my mind.

"*Tell me something I don't know.*"

"*Means we'll put up with whatever we need to. Damien is in trouble. He needs us.*"

Faery spread around us. I focused on breathing, just

breathing. Unleashing my fury on Damien's people would buy me less than nothing. They'd release information in their own sweet time.

Once I knew more, I'd come up with a plan to fix whatever had gone awry.

The doors to the council chamber closed behind us. To my surprise, the room was full of Fae. Pointed ears quivered with outrage. Almond-shaped eyes glared my way.

Hecate's tits. What the hell was I guilty of?

"Remain standing," Logan ordered.

Zeke took up his position by my side.

Maeve walked close. "Damien's been captured," she said. "By the PDA."

"We tried to free him," Logan snarled. "And failed."

I squared my shoulders, enjoying my better than six foot height which made me tower over most of the Fae.

"Tell me where he is. I'll work on it."

"Pfft. Like you can succeed where we failed," Maeve muttered and waved a dismissive hand.

"How about if you don't discount me before I've even left the gate." I held her gaze, not the simplest task.

"Good point," Logan gritted.

I wanted to ask why any of this was my fault, but it didn't matter. What did was pulling Damien out of the jaws of doom. I had no idea what the PDA did to those they captured, but I'd find out soon enough.

Zeke woofed. His signal we should leave.

"Are you coming?" I asked Sita.

The hawk quorked and ruffled her feathers.

"Tell me where he is," I repeated. "So I can get moving."

"We don't like it he selected you as his mate," Logan said, "but in this instance it might work to our advantage."

My mouth flapped open. I shut it fast.

Mate? What the fuck?

Zeke nudged me. In my confusion, I'd missed Maeve's instructions.

"Never mind, I have them," the wolf said and gripped my lower arm in his jaws.

Together, we walked out of the chamber and retraced our steps intent on leaving Faery.

"Where are we going?" I asked Zeke.

A series of images spilled through my mind. My mouth split in half a grin. At least the first part would be straightforward. Best not get too cocky.

Who knew what we'd find in an ironclad compound beneath Seattle's waterfront. To be on the safe side, I put out a call to the Mer people as I loosed my teleport spell. My first stop would be their domain for reinforcements. With witches' affinity for the natural world, we've always gotten along well with sea-dwellers.

Like me, they're not sensitive to iron, and the Fae are their allies.

At least I believe they are. Begged the question why

Logan and Maeve hadn't thought to request aid from that quarter.

Much like my earlier question about what the PDA did to their captives, this one would find an answer sooner rather than later.

Water closed around us as my spell brought us to the Mer people's castle a few hundred yards out to sea. I switched to drawing oxygen from water rather than air and surrounded Zeke and Sita in a bubble.

The glittering shell and stone structure was right in front of me. Lights flickered from several windows courtesy of specialized reflective lichen. I raised a hand and knocked.

"No witches," filtered from somewhere within.

Oh-oh, word of the Coven's association with evil must have spread.

"But I'm one of the good ones," I protested. "Hecate chose me."

The door flew open. A lissome mermaid with aqua scales, matching eyes, long golden hair, and bare breasts examined me.

"So the olden tales are true?"

I nodded. No one had educated me about any "olden tales" regarding Hecate and her plans, but bringing it up would muddy the waters. "They are, and I've come for your aid."

For the second time in an hour, magic analyzed me, cutting deep. I must have passed because the mermaid swam aside, gesturing me in. I ushered the bubble containing Zeke and Sita alongside me. We couldn't remain long; I'd have to be damned convincing pleading my case.

"Are you certain you don't want to send them back to the shore?" The mermaid arched fair brows.

I shook my head. "Someone has it in for me. They're not safe. Neither am I."

"I see. Hurry then. Follow me."

I swam after her, pushing the bubble with Zeke and Sita ahead of me. As we moved deeper into the castle, I organized my thoughts into what I hoped would be a compelling argument. All they needed to know was Damien had been captured. Hopefully, they'd spare me the need for further words and jump in with offers of assistance.

ABOUT THE AUTHOR

Ann Gimpel is a USA Today bestselling author. A lifelong aficionado of the unusual, she began writing speculative fiction a few years ago. Since then her short fiction has appeared in many webzines and anthologies. Her longer books run the gamut from urban fantasy to paranormal romance. Once upon a time, she nurtured clients. Now she nurtures dark, gritty fantasy stories that push hard against reality. When she's not writing, she's in the backcountry getting down and dirty with her camera. She's published over 100 books to date, with several more planned for 2023 and beyond. A husband, grown children, grandchildren, and wolf hybrids round out her family.

Keep up with her at https://www.anngimpel.com or https://www.anngimpelaudiobooks.com

If you enjoyed what you read, get in line for special offers and pre-release special reads. Newsletter Signup!

ALSO BY ANN GIMPEL

SERIES

Alphas in the Wild

Hello Darkness

Alpine Attraction

A Run for Her Money

Fire Moon

Bitter Harvest

Deceived

Twisted

Abandoned

Betrayed

Redeemed

Bound by Shadows

Scarred

Cursed

Promised

Cataclysm

Harsh Line

Warped Line

Cracked Line

Broken Line

Circle of Assassins

Shira

Quinn

Rhiana

Kylian

Grigori

Magick and Misfits

Court of Rogues

Midnight Court

Court of the Fallen

Court of Destiny

Coven Enforcers

Blood and Magic

Blood and Sorcery

Blood and Illusion

Demon Assassins

Witch's Bounty

Witch's Bane

Witches Rule

Dragon Heir

Dragon's Call

Dragon's Blood

Dragon's Heir

Dragon Lore

Highland Secrets

To Love a Highland Dragon

Dragon Maid

Dragon's Dare

Dragon Fury

Earth Reclaimed

Earth's Requiem

Earth's Blood

Earth's Hope

Elemental Witch

Timespell

Time's Curse

Time's Hostage

Gatekeeper

Shadow Reaper

Rebel Reaper

Untamed Reaper

GenTech Rebellion

Winning Glory

Honor Bound

Claiming Charity

Loving Hope

Keeping Faith

Ice Dragon

Feral Ice

Cursed Ice

Primal Ice

Magick and Misfits

Court of Rogues

Midnight Court

Court of the Fallen

Court of Destiny

Rubicon International

Garen

Lars

Soul Dance

Tarnished Beginnings

Tarnished Legacy

Tarnished Prophecy

Tarnished Journey

Soul Storm

Dark Prophecy

Dark Pursuit

Dark Promise

Underground Heat

Roman's Gold

Wolf Born

Blood Bond

Wayward Mage

Hands of Fate

Jinxed

Hunted

Salvaged

Tiana

Wolf Clan Shifters

Alice's Alphas

Megan's Mates

Sophie's Shifters

Wylde Magick

Gemstone

Lion's Lair

Unbalanced

STANDALONE BOOKS

Branded, That Old Black Magic Romance (paranormal romance)

Edge of Night (short story collection, paranormal and horror)

Grit is a 4-Letter Word (nonfiction)

Heart's Flame (post-apocalyptic romance)

Icy Passage (science fiction romance)

Marked by Fortune (post-apocalyptic coming of age story)

Melis's Gambit (historical paranormal romance)

Midnight Magic (paranormal romance)

Red Dawn (post-apocalyptic paranormal romance)

Shadow Play (historical paranormal romance)

Shadows in Time (Highland time travel romance)

Since We Fell (contemporary romance)

Warin's War (paranormal romance)